J. Lang

YOUNG MEN

YOUNG MEN

Stories

Russell Smith

Doubleday Canada Limited

Canadian Cataloguing in Publication Data

Smith, Russell, 1963–
    Young men : stories

ISBN 0-385-25825-9

I. Title.

PS8587.M58397Y68 1999   C813'.54   C98-932854-6
PR9199.3.S64Y68 1999

Jacket photograph by SPL/Deborah Samuels/Photonica
Jacket design by Antoine Moonen
Text design by Janine Laporte
Printed and bound in Canada

Published in Canada by
Doubleday Canada Limited
105 Bond Street
Toronto, Ontario
M5B 1Y3

FRI   10   9   8   7   6   5   4   3   2   1

For Ceri Marsh

Contents

DOMINIC 1

Party Going 3

Young Men 29

Dominic Is Dish 39

LIONEL 71

Desire 73

The Stockholm Syndrome 85

Home 141

JAMES 149

Responsibility 151

Team Canada 165

YOUNG WOMEN 181

Sharing 183

Chez Giovanni 193

Dreams 227

YOUNG MEN

DOMINIC

Party
Going

Sharon is back from Montreal. Dominic thinks about this as he shaves. He calls to Christine, "Will Sharon be there?"

Christine shouts from the back of her closet. He thinks she said yes. He wonders if now is the time to lose the sideburns completely. The razor hovers over his face. His heart is pounding.

Christine comes in in her bra and black pantyhose. She says, "Does my black tunic look silly with the chunky heels?"

"The Fluevogs or the Destroy boots?"

"I can't decide. Or just the patent black Kelianes. They're a little high. We'll be standing."

Dominic shrugs. He glances at her breasts in the mirror. "Push-up bra. PVC skirt and thigh-highs, not pantyhose. My favourite. You'll look great. Any shoes."

Christine puffs out her cheeks and shakes her head. She sits on the edge of the bathtub.

He says, "So they really broke up. I mean she's really broken up."

"Oh yeah. I think it's real."

"Is she here to see Pavel, you think?"

Christine turns her palms upwards. "I don't know. I think she's here to see anyone. She's here to get laid. She already knocked off Eddie Trubashnik, last week."

Dominic cuts himself. *"Jesus."*

"Poor little Eddie." She stands. "I can't decide."

It is incredibly hot and smoky and Dominic's throat is already sore from yelling. The kitchen light is too bright and he is jammed against a countertop by two designers in steely grey who are waving cigarettes too close to his face, and he is yelling at Gabrielle McKendrick and her tall artist friend Sybill who appears to have tattoos all over her: a reptilian tail flicks up her cleavage, a vine snakes around the nape of her neck.

"So this was like the third proposal I'd written," yells Dominic, "and still no money, and I'm starting to think —"

"Bastards," yells Gabrielle.

"Exactly, bastards, and I'm starting to think, Jesus, I hope this show gets picked up, because if not I've just *pissed* away the last three weeks, and —"

"You know Global has the same show in development?" yells Sybill, "I mean similar, you know, the same."

"Bastards," yells Dominic. "Bastards, bastards."

"This is Toronto," yells Gabrielle. "This is Toronto."

He lifts his eyes from the hypnotic shiny curves in Gabrielle's spandex top and sees Julian and Anton, the host, violently kissing in the doorway next to the stove and a bottle about to topple off. He can't see Sharon any more. "Excuse me."

He pushes through to the living room and she is not there

either. He squeezes down the hallway, kissing Karen Trevelyan, who has just arrived and says she wants to talk to him about something when he has a second, and he says okay and steps into a room with a bed piled high with coats. There are four people he has never met standing against the orange walls and laughing and smoking, and Sharon and Christine are sitting, half lying, on the pile of coats. Their heads are close and they are giggling and holding tall narrow glasses. There is a bottle of sparkling wine at Sharon's feet. Both their skirts have ridden up to show their long legs in black tights, shiny and tangled. One strap has fallen off Christine's shoulder. The people along the wall, three men and a woman, are glancing at them, at the bands of naked thigh, the glossy black haircuts. One of the men is staring at Sharon's cleavage and Sharon knows it but is not looking at him.

"*There* you are," calls Sharon. She motions impatiently at Dominic. "Come here, come *over* here. *Sit* with us."

"Come and sit with us, Dominic," says Christine. "We're having fun."

"We are having *so* much fun," says Sharon. "Come and make out with us. I want to make out with both of you."

Dominic sits between them, leaning back uncomfortably in the big soft pile of coats because there is nothing really to support his back. He is on faux fur and wool scarves, all soft and human-smelling. He touches one of his sideburns and then the other. Sharon's hand is on his knee, Christine's in the small of his back. He can smell the wine on their breath. Sharon's lips are slick. "Dominic," she says. "It is *so* good to see you. It is *so* good to see both you guys. I love you guys."

The people in the room turn away from them, trying not to

look. Dominic holds out his glass and Christine fills it with foam, spilling sticky wine on all their knees. They are all laughing too hard.

"Well," says Dominic, "we're making quite a scene."

"Oh, I know," says Sharon. "Who cares. Who gives a fuck."

Sharon's neck and chest are glowing white. He can smell her perfume. He puts his hand on the metallic nylon of Christine's knee. He wants to see what she is thinking, but can't look at her too obviously. Suddenly he has nothing to say. He sips the fizzy wine and starts to hum.

No one says anything.

"Well," says Christine, "we should get going."

When they have their coats on in the crowded hallway, Sharon is still trying to convince them to stay. "Oh come *on*," she says, holding Dominic's lapels with her two hands. "It's *early*."

"I have this thing tomorrow I have to —"

"Sharon," says Christine, laying a hand on her bare shoulder, "whatever you're looking for tonight, you're not going to find here. You should go home."

Sharon scowls and takes her hands off Dominic's coat. "It'll be fun if you *stay* with me, and then we can go home —"

"Sharon," says Dominic, "go home."

In the taxi they don't speak.

Christine says, "What's wrong? Are you pissed off at me?"

"Christ," says Dominic. "What are you talking about?"

"Well what's the matter?"

"*Nothing*, for Christ's sake."

Dominic watches the empty storefronts pass. The salt-stained asphalt is white in the streetlight.

"Look," says Christine, "I couldn't do it. I'm going to be working with her on that Netboy proposal for Bravo, and it would be just too weird. We have to *work* together, right?"

"Listen," says Dominic, "I didn't say *anything*."

She looks out the other window. He knows they are both picturing the long bare thighs, the pale little breasts. He sees Sharon in cafés, on terraces on busy streets, smoking, dark glasses. Montreal. The scent of beer in the streets. Her little white breasts flash in his eyes.

Passing outside, all the dark storefronts are dollar stores, junk stores. They are all closed down.

"And this chick, she looks like — she's got the bleached hair fluffy in front, I just *know* she's got cigarettes in her bag, I'm about to call her Krista or Ashley or —"

"Brandy."

"*Amber* or something, hey, Amber, is Wayne coming over?"

"Hey Amber, going for a smoke?"

"Yeah, jussec, I gotta call my cousin."

"I said to her, Brenda, is Wayne home yet? If he comes home drunk one more time, you gotta get outta there, girl, take the kids —"

"I said, you take the keys from the pickup —"

They are both laughing hard. Sharon's laughter sounds so deep and sunny and natural it makes Dominic think of summer. They are in the viny part of Splat, the dark booths at the back with the wrought-iron sconces in the shape of contorted faces and the twig sculptures everywhere, the stuck-on twigs that wrap around the backs of booths and up the walls like prickly vines the owners have haphazardly seeded, the part Dominic and Christine call "the Jungle." Neither Sharon nor Dominic has mentioned the fact that Dominic asked her here alone or that it must be obvious to her that he waited until Christine was out of town to do so. They have never been out alone before. He tries not to look at the scoop neck of her top, a rubbery top that's cut too low.

Sharon suddenly frowns. "Jesus *fuck* if I see that Dolce and Gabbana coat one more time in this town I'll like *punch* someone."

"And she stamped her little foot."

Her voice goes low. "Oh. My. Fuck."

"What?"

"Don't look now, but Miss Junior P.R. and Marketing over there just got something that looks like a *rye and Coke*, for Chrisake, what's happening to this place, like why do they let them in here? The bartender should at least lecture them."

"It's a travesty. A total goddam travesty. Like, I'm sorry but we have nowhere for you to park your *skidoo* here. I'll tell you something else."

"For free? Don't say for free."

"What?"

"You know how people say, I'll tell ya something *else* for free . . ." She says this in a throaty New York accent.

"What?"

"Forget it. What?"

Dominic gulps at his martini and announces, "Martinis. What the fuck is with these dry martinis. How did this drink become so sophisticated? This is the least sophisticated liquor in the world. Ah, I'll have a glass full of chilled gin, please, because I'm so cool, and a bowl of, I don't know, *gruel*. . ."

"Yes," says Sharon, leaning forward and raising a finger, "but, okay, riddle me this, what's with this row of tequila bottles over the bar? They have a choice of *tequila* here. How many? One, two —"

"Eight," says Dominic with authority. "Eight tequilas at Splat."

"Eight." She taps the tablecloth with a straight white finger. "And anybody who tells you he can tell a difference between tequilas is either a genuine Mexican peasant or he's *lying*. We're talking what you drink when you're a poor fucking campesino who can't afford anything made out of like real food. It's the last of last resorts."

Dominic laughs and looks at the flush on her cheeks as she laughs, her hair glossy as black lacquer, and he feels almost tearful with the desire to say something funnier, to be more beautiful; he feels this desire expanding like a widening hole he is going to fall into; it is dizzying; it spins itself into a tight coil inside him, a hot space, something burning in his chest, a hot metal bar that someone has slipped in there while he was sleeping. He pictures it in his chest cavity, glowing like an ingot that's just been poured. "Ow," he says to no one.

Sharon is suddenly quiet, swirling the Scotch around in her glass. "So," she says, "what's this big thing you wanted to talk about?"

Dominic inhales sharply. "Oh, it's no big thing." He sips his martini. "No big thing at all. I just thought it was rather funny, and I . . . I thought you'd like to hear about this thing I'm working on."

She waits.

"Because it involves you."

She raises her eyebrows.

"It's just this little script I was working on, for a guy at the Film Centre, you know they're always looking for shorts. So it just started as an exercise. Now it looks as if the thing's really going to be produced, and they're looking for festival distribution and everything, and . . . so I thought you should hear about it before you see it." He giggles, and hates himself for it.

She taps her fingers lightly on the tablecloth. He clears his throat. "It's just a little scene. A vignette. There's a couple at a party, they've been going out for quite a while, they spend a lot of time with her best friend, the girl's best friend, I mean the woman's best friend. Anyway. They go to this party."

"Yes."

"And the best friend seems to come on to both of them."

"She does?"

"Well, the guy thinks she does."

"I see." Sharon sits back, stretching her arms out along the back of the banquette. "Go on."

"The guy, of course, would like nothing better than to go home with the friend, but —"

"What's her name?"

"The friend?"

"Yes."

"Ah. Helen. Helena. I haven't decided."

"Okay."

"Anyway, he can't, of course, react to this pass —"

"Is he absolutely *sure* it was a pass?"

Dominic opens his mouth and closes it again. He fumbles for his matches. "Yes," he says. "Yes he's sure it was a pass." He feels sweat squeezing out of the pores on his forehead.

"What if he's wrong?"

Dominic laughs. "He's not wrong. It's my story."

She is quiet but not smiling, staring at the tablecloth.

He goes on. "He can't react to this pass in front of his girlfriend because it's up to her, the girlfriend, whether they do this, go home with her, Helena, because if he says sure, I want to sleep with Helena, his girlfriend will get all uptight and think he's had a crush on Helena all along, you know, but if she says it as a fun thing then it's okay. You know the scene." He shrugs. "But he's just dying for her to say okay, let's go for it, and she doesn't. She's thinking they have to work together —"

"The two of them work together?"

He nods. His face is hot. She is staring at him solemnly, not smiling. "So in the taxi after the party they have this little fight, at least a tense conversation, about it and she realizes he wanted to and she says she can't and he says fine, fine, no problem, but she realizes something is wrong. Because, you see." He stops to light his cigarette. His face is burning. "Because she's right, you see. The girlfriend. He does have a crush on her. On Helena. And he has had all along. For a very long time, anyway."

They are both silent and not looking at each other. Finally, she says, "So what happens?"

He says, "Well. This is the question. How does it end."

She puffs out her cheeks and rubs her face with her palms and he notices her face is red, too. He leans forward and says, "In my little screenplay, it ends with the guy thinking about her all the time. That's all I know. That now he's thinking about her. All the fucking time."

"I see."

Dominic rolls all his life with Christine, the past seven years of his life, into a tight wad in his hand, crumples it up in his grip until he can't feel it except as something outside him, something he could hold on to or throw away, and says, clenching his fist, "It could be a longer story." He tries to smile. "A feature, maybe."

"What *exactly* do you mean?" she says sharply. Her chest is rising and her eyes are bright and hard on him. "I'm not sure what you're suggesting. I'm her closest —"

Dominic raises his palms. "All I'm saying is that there are a couple of possible endings." He counts on his fingers. "It could end there. Nothing could happen. No problem. Everyone could forget all about it and still be friends. Or it could mean the end of the guy's relationship with . . . with Frances is her name. It could totally be the end of that. It could throw his comfortable life totally into disarray and suffering for everybody. Or it could turn into something less —"

"Something secret?" She leans forward, speaking quickly. "Because that's totally impossible. That's totally out of the question."

"Okay. Okay. I guess what I need to know, to know the ending, is what Helena feels for him. For the guy. Whether she feels anything at all."

Sharon puts both palms to her cheeks as if checking for fever. She stares at his martini glass and frowns. Nobody says anything. He is waiting for her to put her white hand down on the floral cloth so that he can put his over it and feel its heat or cool, he doesn't know. Nobody moves.

"But that's the thing about groovy Duncan and the groovy Digmeisters and Bob, too, for that matter, and the Jalapeños and all the other pop groups we know, everything about the culture they aspire to, and I mean *everything*, they learned from television. It's not theirs and it's not valuable, either, it's American junk culture. It's like advertising music. And I've never understood the glamour of the South, why they all want to pretend they're black sharecroppers or whatever, or the West either, why they all want to be cowboys or driving big beat-up cars on desert highways, the road movie, the tequila and gambling culture, I just don't see it as attractive at all."

Sharon yawns and rolls over onto him, rubbing her cheek across his bare chest. Her black hair washes over his skin. He smiles and looks at the sunlight patterned by the leaves outside, wavering blotches on her bedroom wall, against the subtle beige-and-white stripe pattern she did with endless hours of masking tape and washes. It still smells of paint, a clean smell. The light shimmers on the hardwood, over the white duvet. He stretches; he is warm and his muscles are still. Her hair is heavy on his chest. He knows she is not interested in his rant on popular music, but he is talking for himself, thinking that maybe he could turn this into an essay, sell it to *Haze* or *Random*, they love opinion stuff like that, get a couple of hundred bucks for it. He hopes he remembers the idea, and to talk to Brotman about it. He rolls her onto her side and rolls on his side so their chests are touching. He cups one breast with his hand and she quivers. He kisses her forehead; it is cool.

He had not thought she would always smell so faint and cool, like the sea, even when they were shiny with sweat. He had not been able to imagine her skin's scent at all, before.

"*Fuck*," they both say simultaneously, as the car stereo in the alley outside her window wakes again with an apocalyptic boom. The windowpane rattles; they can feel the bed humming with every thud; it sounds subterranean, as if something very large is clawing its way towards the surface of the earth from deep in the rock. They hear the teenage boys shouting at each other over the noise; they cover their heads with pillows.

"*Fuck*, Luis, crank it, man," says Dominic in a hoarse voice. "I mean I really want you to crank up the thump, man."

"You see Hernando take out that mangiacake, man?" says Sharon. "One fucking crack, man, right on the jaw, the guy goes down like, *wham*."

"Fucking unreal, man, that guy is fucking awesome, man. You gonna see that chick Maria?"

"Aw, man, that chick is a fucking *hairpin*, man, she won't stop calling me up, I had to tell my mother, I said 'Ma, if she calls here again, I swear I'm not here —'"

"I said, 'Ma, I swear to the Virgin I'll clear all those bikes out of the garage, I told you, they're Joey's, not mine, yeah, sure he paid for them—'"

"Don't ask too many questions, Ma."

They're laughing again; this is their favourite skit since Sharon found this apartment in the Portuguese district, which is the price she pays for having so pretty a place for so cheap. Their noses are touching; he is breathing her breath. He slides his hand down between her legs and finds it still wet and warm; he stiffens again. She gasps and they are silent for a minute.

She whispers, "How many times do you think we've fucked?"

He thinks. "Two boxes? Almost. A box and a half."

"Not bad."

"Not bad for three weeks, and just Tuesday and Friday afternoons. And Wednesday mornings."

"The odd Sunday evening choir practice."

"Choir practice!" He giggles, and then suddenly they both go quiet and still. He knows it was a mistake to laugh. She lets go of his penis.

"Sorry."

Very quietly, she says, "It's awful."

He sighs, puffs out his cheeks, throws off the pillow on his head. His penis subsides. He rolls onto his back. He looks at his watch. "Fuck."

She digs her head further under her pillow.

"I'd better go."

Her voice is muffled. "What time does she get home?"

"Five. But it could be early. I'd like to be there before four-thirty."

She says nothing. He gets up and begins hunting for his clothes. She sits up, hugs a pillow to her chest. She says, "This is terrible, and something has to happen, one way or the other."

"I know that."

"We're going to get caught. And I can't take it. You have to make a decision."

"I know that. I *know* that. I know *that*. Okay? It's just hard. It's harder than you think. I'm sorry."

"And even if someone else finds out then she'll find out and then she'll think everybody knew and we were just laughing at her all along. It's terrible. It's, it's . . . *rude* is what it is. And I'm not like this. I'm not a bad person. I can't believe I'm doing this."

Dominic tries to breathe deeply. He can't find his underwear. "Don't be silly, you're not a bad person, this was just a . . . Listen. Okay. It's a difficult thing to do. Seven years. It's seven years of my life. And I need time to think this through, time alone. And I'm going to be in New York next week. It will be clearer there, when I'm away from . . . from everyone. I'll make a decision. I promise."

"Great. So I just have to sit here and wait for what you decide."

He sits on the bed. "I know it's terrible, and I'm sorry. But I just can't do this really fast. You wouldn't be able to either."

She drops her head. "No."

"And while it's going on, I understand if you don't, if you don't want to . . ."

"To what?"

"To stick around. I mean nothing is forcing you to . . ." He feels a faint nausea. "To wait for me to decide."

She is silent for a moment. "I know. I shouldn't."

In a quiet voice, he says, "I just hope you do." He gets up and finds his shirt, his jacket.

She says, "I don't even want you to go to New York."

He laughs.

"How long will you be gone for?"

"Five days."

"I don't want you to go."

He laughs again. "Just five days. You'll last." He pulls his underwear from under the bed.

She watches him dress. "Aren't you going to take a shower?"

"I guess. Yeah. Okay."

She is still clutching her pillow to her like protection. He stops to look at her: her cheeks are pink, her hair loose on her shoulders.

"You look beautiful," he says.

"What would you say if she caught you?"

"How would she catch me?"

"Say you forgot to take a shower, or didn't have time or something, and she smelled me on you. What would you tell her?"

"I've been thinking about that." He sits on the bed, his back to her.

"I don't think any old lie would work. I think she could guess I'd been fucking someone. So I'd confess, I'd tell her I've been having an affair."

"With me?"

"No. I'd make someone up. It would hurt her, it would kill her, and we'd probably break up, but it still wouldn't be as bad as if she knew it was you."

Sharon is silent. Then she says, "Who would you make up?"

He shrugs. "Somebody young, not serious. Somebody I could say was just a fling. It wouldn't hurt her so much. Like a student. One of those girls who hung around after I gave my talk at the Young Directors thing. A film student."

"An eager film student."

"Yeah. At, like, Carleton or York."

"No, a community college film program. Like Sheridan."

"She's in animation at Sheridan."

They both laugh. She says, "What's her name?"

"I'll refuse to give her her name."

"But you'll have to know it. For yourself."

He considers. "Something not too crass. She'd better be at least cool, my film student."

"Clara?" She knows he loves this name.

He smiles. "Or even more over the top. She's a little wild. Irina. Georgiana. Carmen. Big hair, red lips. One parent is Spanish. Her father. Who is a diplomat. So she's lived all over the world."

"I'm getting jealous of your film student."

"She wears tight red dresses and —"

"*Red* dresses? I'm not jealous any more."

"No, no, she's just verging on tacky but not quite; more like fey-dramatic, you know?"

"Like she wears essential oils?"

"Or at least Opium, you know, you smell her a mile away."

Sharon giggles. "She has a fake English accent she slips into sometimes when she's nervous —"

"Which she picked up on a summer program at Oxford University."

"And she rides a bicycle painted with flowers, that she did herself —"

"Of course. And big straw hats in the summer —"

"And a wicker basket. *Yuck!*"

Dominic laughs, turns, wraps his arms around her neck and pushes her down onto the bed. She writhes, reaches for his penis. He lies on top of her, naked, breathing hard, and says, "Hey, don't be too hard on her, she's only young. She doesn't have your wisdom. Your experience."

She locks her eyes with his. She spreads her arms on the pristine cotton and opens her legs. She touches the tip of his tongue with the tip of her tongue. Her eyes are burning into his. The bass from the alley booms.

Christine is screaming. She is silhouetted in their kitchen window, standing. She is screaming, "You fucking bastard. You fucking bastard," through tears. Her face is red and twisted. Dominic sits hunched on the living-room sofa, looking through the archway at her. He clutches a cushion to his chest, the way he has watched Sharon do. His guts are heaving; he thinks he will be sick. His head is buzzing as if he has taken ten antihistamines. He pictures himself standing in the dock at the war crimes tribunal with the television cameras on him: Did you massacre those Muslim villagers? Yes, sir, I did, I killed all those women and children, I can't remember why, I have no idea why I did it. He feels everything inside him draining out, dripping out of all his pores until he is a sucking black plastic airbag, the kind beside the operating table in old hospital movies. He bows his head, stiffens his shoulders against the words which pound him like boulders. He hides his face in the cushion.

"Wasn't that Gabrielle McKendrick?"

"Yes."

"Did she see you?"

"Yes."

"Oh." They are walking bravely hand in hand right down College Street, in raincoats (hers beige linen, his dove-grey gabardine); it is early spring. The streets are wet and windy. It was Sharon's idea to come here. She said they had to reclaim it, stake it out, like dogs pissing around a yard, which made Dominic laugh.

"Well. That was odd, then."

"Maybe she didn't see me."

"We both looked right at her."

Dominic is silent.

"I even heard you say hi."

"Don't worry about it. Forget it."

They walk another block, but they have let go of each other's hands. Then Dominic says, "Let's go down Clinton."

Walking down Clinton, he says, "She never did like me." A sudden gust of wind makes them duck their heads. They button their coats as they walk.

Finally Dominic says, "It would be nice if it were warm."

"We could sit outside at cafés."

He knows what she is thinking. "On Prince Arthur. St. Denis."

"The Carré Saint Louis."

"It's probably raining there too."

She sighs. "I know. And there's no work."

He says, "Why don't we call someone up tonight? Have some people over." He adds, "At your place," quickly, to stress that it is still her place, even though he has been living there for three weeks, his old duffel bags and newspaper-wrapped frames stuffed into her study. He is going to find his own place, although he hasn't been looking very hard.

"Who could we call?"

"Well. Michael and Lizzie?"

She puffs out her cheeks. "I hardly know them. And they're *married.*"

"I could try Alison again."

"She didn't call you back last time."

They walk on, turn on to the sullen strip of Portuguese body shops on Dundas, the fading travel agencies. He takes her hand again. "We could rent a video."

Sharon unhooks the big glass frame that hangs over her bed, the bright fish print that Colin did at art school and that she always hangs over her bed wherever she moves. She begins taping newspaper over it. Dominic, watching from the windowsill, feels sick. The shiny hardwood floor is littered once again with newspaper, boxes. He wipes sweat from his face. It is hot, over thirty degrees, and humid; the sky is yellow with haze. Two car stereos are competing in the alley, as if bashing each other with invisible tree trunks. He has to yell for her to hear him. "I still can't believe this," he yells. "I think it's crazy."

"We've been through this."

"You just haven't given it a chance. You still haven't heard back from *Random* about the cooking show spin-off, you haven't tried —"

"I don't *like* it here."

"Well neither do I, neither does anyone, but there just isn't anything else, is there? I mean, what the fuck are you going to do back there once the Synapse contract expires, I mean there's a very good chance the show will get cancelled, and aside from that there's —"

"If you don't like living somewhere." She stands up. "You shouldn't live there. Right? And if you don't like it here you should leave too." She looks at him and her face twists. "All you have to do is come with me."

Dominic suddenly feels so unbearably hot he wants to rip off his T-shirt, and almost does, but he fears he smells bad, and does not want to reveal his torso in daylight. He swings his arms instead. He breathes in and says, "As you say, we've been through that. You know I can't leave the Axiom gig, it's too stable, and now the feature project really looks like it might have Pyramid on —"

She has turned, is gathering up more newspaper.

Dominic can't watch. He turns to the window to see the boys pushing each other on the concrete. He can never tell if they are playing or fighting — a problem he has with dogs, too. He tries to imagine packing his stuff: it would be easy, as he gave up all the furniture, has not unpacked most of it anyway. He imagines calling Kuzscinsky, quitting the teaching job, and feels sicker. He couldn't deal with Pyramid all the way from Montreal, he'd get forgotten, vanish from everybody's minds like a lost computer file.

From behind him, he hears Sharon sniffling. He wants to put his hands over his ears. He can't turn around. He can't move.

Karen Trevelyan is having a party. So far Dominic has avoided everyone's parties (except the married people's, where he can be sure not to run into anyone), and he has heard that Christine has been avoiding the same parties, which is silly, as no one gets to go to any parties that way. If he goes to this one and sees her there, it means she has made a decision to risk seeing him as well, which would mean they were both in the same position, after eight months, which would interest him.

He opens his wine in the kitchen as slowly as he can, delays his entrance into the living room.

She stands with a man and a woman he has not met. She wears a cool crushed velvet suit, long and slim, really cool, something he had not thought she could have pulled off. Her hair has gone blonder, longer, is tied back. His heart pounds.

She sees him and he tries a smile. She hesitates for a second, stiffens, then shrugs and smiles wearily. He is relieved.

Soon they are sitting alone. He is surprised to hear about her contract with Pyramid. In fact, he is jealous of anyone with a job. His own work has not been going so well lately; the feature languishes, even the Film Centre short fell through. He has had to borrow money this month.

He tells her this, tells her seriously that things are not going well. She listens with interest. He tries to look deflated. He is glad he is not as well dressed as he could be; he thought at length about this before coming. Then he says, "You look great. You look *terrific.*"

She says, "Thank you." Then, "You are a fucking bastard."

He laughs uncertainly. "I know." He looks down humbly.

She laughs too, shakes her head; then he laughs for real, and they clink their glasses, laughing. She crosses and uncrosses her velvet legs. He can smell her scent, a new scent, sharp and pretty.

"German and slow or Hong Kong and violent?"

"Those are my only options?"

"Well, nothing about sisters, or mothers and daughters, at least. Or trios of close schoolgirls. None of that. And no plight of the oppressed, no Nicaraguan resistance or like Chinese women, okay? Those are my only parameters. I would take French sentimental, in a pinch, or lush period English, if pushed."

They walk arm in arm down College Street towards Content Video. It is fall again; Christine wears her brown suede jacket. He knows they look striking. He knows she will not fight his choice of video, but they go through this discussion out of politeness. They have been very nice to each other, intensely kind, since it started again, so tentatively, in the heat. The cool has bonded them somewhat, solidified it. And he can be firm when things are important, like this. "But my ideal would be grey impenetrable German or Polish."

She is not paying attention, looking across the street at the plate-glass window of Hunger, which irritates him, even though he is pleased to have his way on the video, for he would like some semblance of dissent, a show of fight before the triumph. He wonders which would be better, to have her seriously opinionated on film, a rival — like Sharon, he thinks suddenly, and for the first time in weeks — or to have sole control, watch whatever he wanted, forever free of sad Soweto mothers and irritating Australian schoolgirls.

And there she is, Sharon, stepping out of Hunger in a black leather jacket; it is what Christine was looking at.

"Fuck," she says.

"Fuck," he says.

"Fuck is she doing here."

"All right."

"Do we have to talk to her?"

"For Christ's sake, of course we — she's seen us."

Sharon is crossing the street. She seems confident, says, "Hi guys," without blushing. Her face has had sun. Not tanned; she is too pale for that; but glowing.

"Hello," says Dominic heartily. "What are you in town for?"

They do the small talk, in the face of Christine's silence. Sharon avoids looking at either of them while she talks; she scans the street. Yes, the Synapse show was cancelled, but she has a pretty good waitressing job, and is working on her feature script — partly in a creative writing course she's taking, eventually part of an MFA. She's not in town for business, just visiting. She's full of warm congratulations on Christine's job at Pyramid, Dominic's full-time teaching position, the new house.

"Good for you, though," says Dominic, sincerely. He had forgotten what she looked like. And he has never seen her wear second-hand clothes before; it is very Montreal. Heavy black boots, bare legs. It is painful. He tells her he is surprised she can't find film work, there aren't more American M.O.W.'s being shot in Montreal; things seem to be jumping again here, honey wagons blocking every intersection. She shrugs as if she doesn't think about it much. She keeps looking over his shoulder, as if expecting someone.

He wishes he weren't wearing a stupid professorial tweed jacket just because Christine said she liked it. He feels ugly.

He wants to ask her if she is seeing anyone, and would do it if they were alone.

She only looks at him directly once, in a moment of silence, and he sees her eyes grow big again, as if with fright. He wants to speak to her alone and he knows that she does too. She winces and looks away; for a second it looks like pain.

And she just goes away. She says, bravely and directly, "Bye, Christine, nice to see you," to which Christine must mutter, "Bye, Sharon," and Dominic must watch her legs and the short skirt stride away. He wants to know what is going on in Montreal, what art cinemas are functioning, where the booze-cans are, but he hasn't permitted himself to think about that for some time. He imagines Sharon having meetings in the café at the Cinéma Parallèle, the coffee smell and chin stubble, the laziness, her rushing in late with a bouquet of flowers she has to give to some girlfriend who is sick, someone who works in a restaurant and doesn't know anyone at Pyramid and doesn't care, someone who is having an unhappy affair with some tall South American guy — indeed, this is the guy Sharon is meeting, a beautiful guy with long hair who makes films in French and Spanish.

He knows he is being ridiculous.

It takes them several blocks before Christine unfreezes and says something, something conciliatory like, "Well, that wasn't too bad," and Dominic won't talk about it, he just notes that Pianissimo has a new menu, seems to have gone upscale, which is obscurely disappointing.

French words are welling in his head, out of nowhere: *Un express, s'il vous plaît. Un demi pression.*

There are barrows of rotting leaves in the gutters.

Avi and Alison stop to chat; they are getting married.

Il n'y en a pas, monsieur. Il n'a pas d'âme. Artistique. Artisanat. Idiotisme. Christine's arm grips his like a hasp. They go into the video store, where he is safe.

Young
Men

"So." Dominic looked across the table at Gordon. Gordon smiled at him. He wore dark glasses, in which Dominic could see his own tiny, warped reflection. Dominic was also wearing dark glasses. They were both wearing linen shirts which fluttered slightly in the breeze. King Street rustled around them; it seemed full of women in dresses.

"So," said Gordon. "How are you?"

"I'm good. It's good to see you."

"It's good to see you too. I just thought I'd call because —"

"Oh, of course, it's great to —"

"Just to see how you —"

"Would you gentlemen care for something to start?"

"Are you going to have something?" asked Dominic.

Gordon looked at his watch. "I have to be back at the office."

"I'll have a soda with lime," said Dominic.

Gordon said, "Do you have a fumé blanc by the glass?"

"Ah . . ." The waitress's blue eyes wandered over them. "I'm not sure."

"Could you check for me?" said Gordon quietly.

"What I do have, which is similar, sir, is a Pinot Grigio, which is a little fruitier, but I find it —"

"You've had it?"

"I like it." She smiled, and Dominic had to look away from her bare neck and smooth bust. "Shall I get you a —"

"I'll have a glass of Chardonnay, whatever you have, the *biggest* you have," said Gordon, passing her the wine list with the tips of his fingers as if he didn't even want to touch it. "Something oaky, something I can chew on. I trust you." He smiled at her from behind his glasses.

Dominic resented not having ordered a drink; he felt cheated. He almost called her back as she swung away, but hesitated too long. He resented the feeling, distant as a hangover, that he still wasn't quite sure of the rules.

"Attractive," said Gordon.

"Terrific, in fact," said Dominic. "Monster. I'd forgotten what it was like, downtown. Stuck up in the frozen north." He had been teaching at a university in a suburb.

"It's particularly wonderful today." They both looked over the railing — they were practically right in the middle of the sidewalk — at the suits, walking quickly past them, and the folded newspapers and the bare legs. It was one of the first days warm enough for them. The breeze was enough to make Dominic shiver. A streetcar rumbled past and drowned something that Gordon said. Gordon took his cellphone from his pocket and laid it on the table.

"So," said Dominic.

"So," said Gordon. "How was it?"

"The teaching?"

"Well, everything. You got a lot of thinking done too, I suppose?"

"Oh, more than that. I got a couple of my own projects finished."

"Really? Did you? Well, that's good. That's terrific. And you have any, you have any definite plans for them?"

"Oh yes."

There was a silence.

"Good." Gordon looked at the menu. "I always enjoy the carpaccio. I like a *wet* carpaccio."

"So do I. It's wet?"

"Wettish."

"The duck crêpe with wasabe cream looks good."

"Actually, I'd warn you off that one."

"Ah."

"The crêpe is heavy. Stodgy."

"Forget it. I'll have the carpaccio too."

"Let's start with that and decide on mains later."

"Fine." They folded their menus and smiled at each other's glasses. "So how are *you*?" said Dominic.

"Actually," said Gordon, "I'm good. Very good. A number of . . . a number of things on the go."

"Excellent. Are you still at —"

"Well, for the time being, yes."

"Ah?"

"Yes. Something — a possibility has just presented itself to go somewhere else. It looks like a pretty sure thing. You understand that I can't be specific just yet about what it —"

"No no, of course, no no no. But you're happy — excited about it?"

"Oh yes. It would be a pretty interesting position. As I say,

things are just about to be finalized, and I'll let you know as soon
as I know for *sure*, and actually, I probably will want to talk to you
then, because there are ways in which you might be able to, to —"

"To get involved."

"To contribute. In some way. Yes. This is one of the reasons I
wanted to see you, to just touch base with you, see what you were
up to, see if you had any projects on the go, if you were looking to
get involved with any —"

"Oh, I'm always looking to get involved," said Dominic.

"Good."

"Have you gentlemen decided?"

Gordon opened his mouth but Dominic spoke as quickly as he
could. "We'll have two carpaccios to start, please. And we'll order
the mains later."

"All righty then." She leaned to gather the menus.

"Could we hang on to those?" said Dominic.

"Oh. Certainly." She was looking around as if someone was
going to catch her.

"Since we haven't decided yet."

"Of course." She was still hesitating. "I'll just leave these with
you then."

"That's what I'm getting at," said Dominic, and Gordon snorted. Dominic felt a wave of guilt like sudden nausea, but he smiled
at Gordon.

As she swished away, Gordon said, "Her boss has told her
never to leave the menus."

"Isn't that tough?" said Dominic, and felt it again.

"Isn't it. So." Gordon took a sip of his white wine. The glass
was large, round and yellow with wine, misty with condensation.

"You know, that looks so good I think I might have a drink after all." Dominic looked around for the tall girl.

Gordon was frowning. "That's not exactly what *I'd* call oaky." He swallowed again and grimaced. "You know," he said, his voice deep with concern, "I'm not even sure that's a Chardonnay at all."

"Excuse me," said Dominic to the girl as she passed. "I'm sorry, I've changed my mind. I'll have a glass of wine too."

"Don't order this one," said Gordon, just so she could hear, and Dominic cringed again

"I'll be right with you," she said. She was carrying plates of food.

"Anyway," said Dominic. "So."

"So. How's life otherwise? On the personal front, I mean."

"Well, you heard I — me and Christine are no more."

"Yes, I heard that. I'm sorry to hear it. Was that . . . tough?"

"Yes, it was."

"That's too bad."

Another streetcar passed, so they didn't have to talk about it for a second. Finally Gordon said, "But I suppose it's better in the long run?"

"Oh yes. Much."

"Good." Gordon drank from his glass and grimaced again. "You know, I don't think this is what I ordered at all."

"Well, you did say you trusted her," said Dominic gently.

"I didn't trust her to give me a goddam Riesling or something. Hello."

"What can I get you?" She was at their side again, blushing a little, Dominic thought, but perhaps he was being optimistic. He studied her flawless skin.

"I'd like a glass of the Pinot Grigio you mentioned, and my friend —"

"Are you sure that's not what you brought *me*?" said Gordon.

She hesitated. "I'm sure that's the Chardonnay, sir. You don't like it?"

"I don't think it's a Chardonnay, but never mind. Let me try something else."

"Certainly." She shook her head slightly to clear a wisp. It was very controlled. "What would you like?" Her voice had a fine edge now; it was crisper.

"I'd *like* a fumé blanc, but I guess I'll have to —"

"There's a sauvignon blanc, a Pinot Grigio, and another Chardonnay, it's from Oregon, it's a little lighter, so —"

While this went on, Dominic stared at Gordon's cellphone, lying flat and small and heavy and meaningful on the table, as if it was threatening to ring, a silent threat to everyone around.

"Anyway," said Gordon, once she had gone. "Whatever happened to that project you had going with Pyramid?"

"Oh, Pyramid, that just, they really —" Dominic shook his head. "Fizzled out?"

"I think they kind of took me for a ride." He sighed. Suddenly he was tired of caution. "They read my proposal, liked it, brought me in, I had all kinds of meetings, and then it was like everybody forgot about it all of a sudden, as if nothing had ever happened." Dominic squeezed his napkin into a ball. The waitress was weaving towards them.

"Who were you dealing with there, if you don't mind my asking?"

"Not at all. Mimi Bean."

"Ah. Mimi Bean." Gordon leaned back, smiling widely.

"What? You know her?"

"I've had similar dealings with her."

Dominic felt exasperated. He leaned forward. "Well *what?* Tell me what you know about her."

"Pinot Grigio," said the waitress, "and the Eyrie Vineyards Chardonnay. Are you finished with the first one, sir? I'm so sorry you didn't like it. We won't charge you for this one, sir."

"*Thank* you," said Gordon, as if to a small child. He smiled up at her like a grandmother. Dominic half expected him to pat her on the head. He wondered what Gordon had that made people react to him like this. Even he, Dominic, wanted Gordon to be pleased all the time.

Absently, she began to gather the menus again.

"If you don't mind," said Dominic.

"Oh, of course," she said. "I'm sorry."

He watched her hips slice the air in their tight black fabric and felt a sudden bitterness, at her, at Gordon. "Nice girl," he said, "but obviously not blessed with vast intellect."

Gordon laughed loudly. He threw his napkin onto the table and laughed some more.

Dominic blushed with his own success.

"Listen," said Gordon. "Did you ever have the impression that Mimi Bean's motivation, in her dealings with you, did you ever have the suspicion that her motivations weren't entirely professional?"

"You mean, that her motivations may have been more social than professional?"

"So to speak."

"Did I ever feel that she might have just wanted to —"

"To bag you. So to speak."

Dominic laughed. "That's exactly what I thought. I thought it was my self-flattering imagination."

Gordon shook his head, leaned forward, and in a murmur began to tell him stories of Mimi Bean. Dominic listened closely, his heart pounding. This was the exciting part of being with Gordon. This was really lunch, this was really lunch on King Street. As Gordon spoke and chuckled, and he chuckled too, he watched the women passing on the sidewalk, brushing past him in envelopes of perfume, and felt that he was watching them *knowingly*, and thought that he might even try, today, before the end of lunch even, to smile at one.

"But I'll tell you one thing you may not have noticed, in case you ever *do* need to know," said Gordon, finishing up. His voice went even lower. "She's a little heavy in the leg."

"Ah." Dominic raised his eyebrows.

"Dresses very carefully. You'd never notice. But she's a little heavy in the leg."

"Thank you." They both nodded sagely and sipped their wine. The wine tasted marvellous. Dominic felt marvellous. He knew their linen shirts looked great together. When the waitress came back, he would not be afraid to make some crack about the menus and her boss watching, or even about the wine. He glanced at a woman on the sidewalk who had a white skirt and top on, and blonde hair; she carried a bunch of flowers. He pushed his glasses down and caught her eye. She stared for a second, and he smiled, as confidently as he could. She quickly looked away and quickened her pace as she passed, as if she had seen something that frightened her.

Dominic Is Dish

Dominic burped quietly in the back of the cab, checking his watch. The darkness outside was thickening as downtown slipped away. They were on the expressway, and then under it, gliding between lanes and sudden flares in a tunnel as aggressive as a video game, and then among factory buildings and orange parking lots. He wished he had eaten dinner instead of a beer and a handful of sweet-and-hot bar snacks. But it had been too early for dinner. When he got back it would be too late.

The cab slowed as the driver tried to make out street signs. There didn't seem to be any street signs. Indeed, the street itself seemed to have swelled into an infinite terrain of cracked concrete; perhaps they were driving across a parking lot. Bars of orange slid across Dominic's face in the back seat; he shrank into the corner to avoid them. He was enjoying the feeling of being invisible.

The car came to a stop. "Is *East* Consumers Boulevard, yes?"

Dominic arched his back to lift his bum off the seat to untrap his coat pocket and the uncomfortable lump under his thigh. He extracted the object. "Just a minute." He held it, a glass salt shaker, up to the window. "Can you pull forward into the light a little?"

The car crept into an orange cone. Dominic squinted at the salt shaker, rotating it in his fingers. It was a regular restaurant-issue eight-sided salt shaker with a chrome top. There were transparent words somehow imprinted or engraved on the glass, forming a sentence which wrapped around. Dominic squinted and read, "Seventeen ninety-one Consumers Boulevard East, at . . . just a minute . . ." The lamplight split into diamonds in the prism of glass. "Looks like Service Road. Is there a road called Service Road?"

The driver nodded, and they were moving again. "Service Road, yes. I know."

Dominic burped.

They got back on a road and crossed some railway tracks and stopped again at a chain-link gate which was open and led to a parking lot which was crowded with people. There were television trucks and bright lights on poles. "This is it," said Dominic. "May I have a receipt, please?"

He stepped out into the cold and pulled his coat around him. The cab rumbled away and he hesitated before walking towards the parking lot. The building was a cone-shaped salt storage hangar with a gaping truck entrance. He could see inside to a bright space with rows of chairs.

He looked up and down the road, as deserted as a rural highway. Incredibly, there was a payphone, coldly glowing at a distant intersection. He walked towards it in the silence, thinking that he should have done up the buttons on his coat but that he was almost at the phone and there would be a door he could close. It turned out it was a modern one with a phone stuck to a pole under a light and no booth.

He tried to button his coat as he dialled.

He got her answering machine and said, "Hello, hello, hello, hello, hello, hello, hello, hello, hello," until she answered.

"Hello?"

"It's me."

"Hi."

"I'm here, I found the place."

"Oh."

"It's way the hell in the middle of nowhere."

"Uh-huh."

"But," he said, "I mean it's not hard to get here by cab. It cost about fifteen bucks but if you wanted to come, I would pay. Just get a receipt."

There was a television in the background.

"Leyalla?"

"Yeah, I don't think I'll come."

"It might be really good for you, I mean your career and all. Lots of people you might want to meet, all the editors and photographers —"

"No, I can't. I have to . . ."

Another cab hissed past, two white faces in the back. They looked like Danny Fineman from the daily paper and Judith Gall from *Awe*, but he couldn't be sure. "Leyalla? You have to what?"

"I have to do something."

"Oh. Okay. I'll be home pretty soon, though, I won't stay if there's a party afterwards. So I can just meet you at my place?"

"Ah. Sure. Okay."

"Okay. Look, I really wish I didn't have to —"

"Dominic, do you think you can mention my name to that lady at *Awe*, Judith whatsername? I hear they're looking for stylists."

"Sure. In fact I think I just saw her."

"And maybe you can remind the guy from the paper that he has my portfolio?"

"Sure. I'll drop your name wherever I can. But that kind of thing — it would really be better if I could introduce you myself."

There was a short pause. "Well, it's really not that much to ask."

"Sure, sure," said Dominic quickly, "I don't mind at all, I'm just saying, I'm just, never mind. It's no problem."

"Thanks."

"Okay, then. I'll see you at home. At my place. Just let yourself in. Okay?"

"Okay." Her voice was faint.

"In about two hours. Maybe three."

"Okay. Have a good —"

"Listen, Leyalla, I'm really sorry about this. I really have to do this one, though, since I'm filling in for Trini this week on this thing, and you know, the whole crowd will be here. It's just work. But I really wish we, I wish . . ." He stopped, feeling awkward. "I wish we could be spending more time together."

No response.

He cleared his throat. "I really wish . . . I'm sorry I can't be with you."

She laughed, short and hard. "I think," she said, "I'll be able to take care of myself."

Dominic walked through the crowd in the parking lot and the security guys with their black headsets. A videographer was interviewing Amanda Crisp from the fashion section of *Edge;* she stood in an arc of white light. Dominic flapped his hand and winked at her as he passed, and she said, "I'm really excited about seeing a young designer take some — hi, sweetie — initiative, and this is one of the things we've come to expect from the Conceptor program . . ."

Dominic smiled at her smile, and then he smiled at Vibica Ashe and shook Franco Fiorelli's hand and moved towards the huge hangar doorway and its promise of spotlights, feeling himself grow in importance and popularity with every stride: here he was known. Two enormous men barred the entrance, one black, one white, their hands on their hips; they wore black sweatshirts marked "SECURITY" in block letters as yellow as the streetlamps; they wore black caps on backwards, they wore headsets with microphones, they carried long tubular black flashlights, they folded their arms and looked at Dominic. "Invitation, sir."

Dominic did not look at them; he nudged little Bob Minor who stood next to them in a many-buttoned tweed suit and a lavender shirt and a sky-blue tie under his Arctic Bear Extreme Cold Parka and who looked up from his clipboard and said, "*Dominic!* How *are* you?"

Dominic grinned. "Bob. Good to see you."

"Good to see *you!*" Into his headset microphone, Bob Minor said, "Leezie, honey, are these doors open or not? There are so many people inside already we might as well — well, it's going to have to be fast, Leezie, we're talking five minutes *max*, okay? So let's get on it, everybody. Dominic, I'm so glad you could *come!* Now you're with — just a minute . . ." Bob Minor tore through pages on his clipboard. "I've put you with Danny from the paper and Judith from *Awe*, you're fifty-three through fifty-seven, on the right side, is that okay? You're all friends and everything still, right? One never knows."

"Perfect," said Dominic. "No problem."

"Now who are you writing for these days?"

"Oh, everybody. Freelance, you know."

Bob Minor frowned, looking at his clipboard.

"I've done some things for *Buzzer* lately, in the fashion section, which must be why you invited me."

"*Buzzer*, hey?" Bob Minor looked up at him with a little smile.

A queue was already forming behind Dominic; he could smell the perfume hanging in the frozen air. The security men were shifting uneasily, staring at him. "Yeah." He smiled too, a little nervously.

"You wouldn't be the guy who writes Dish, would you?"

Dominic laughed, shaking his head. "I wish. I only wish." He tried to sound sad. "No such glamour for me."

"Whoever it is has said some very nasty things about us. Mister Rudix Posure, very funny. I *shouldn't*," said Bob Minor, smiling demurely, "even let you in!"

"Bob," said Dominic, "what's a show without me?" And he winced, for he hated talking like that.

"What indeed. You didn't bring a guest?"

"No. She couldn't come. Last minute."

"That's too bad," said Bob Minor, crossing out a line on his clipboard. "I wish you could let us know in advance, this sort of thing, Dom, you know how many tickets we —"

"Sorry, Bob. Last-minute thing." Dominic stepped forward, smiling up at the security men's faces; they cast very brief questioning glances at Bob Minor before stepping aside. He slipped through them as if through elevator doors, and they closed silently again behind him. Dominic let out a breath, releasing his grip on the salt shaker in his pocket. It was always a victory when you didn't have to show an invitation.

The first thing he noticed inside the hangar was that it was cold; just as cold as the air outside. He looked up at the soaring dome roof, vaulted like a cathedral. The space was perfectly circular; the floor was concrete; the air smelled of diesel oil. There were two raised runways, crossing at the centre, and rows of chairs along each one, with a printed name tag on the seat of each chair. He shivered and then saw the bar table covered in white cloth with uniformed waiters against the far wall; there was already a cluster of black coats there.

He almost broke into a run crossing the room. He restrained himself. Faces turned as he approached the bar: Danny and Judith.

"Well well well, darling, mister very *very* suave, intellectuals only here, give us a kiss, *mwa* —"

"Danny sir, loved the piece on — *mwa* — the handgun chic thing, very vicious, very very *very* —"

"Dominic, sir, I haven't seen you since at least last night and I love you and you and you, I am not serious enough for you, sir, you *Buzzer* types, we only talk TV here —"

"*Love* your *coat*," said Dominic, "what is it, that new nylon with —"

"Brushed cotton, with a latex seal," said Danny, "cool, eh?"

"And look at *you*," said Judith, "let me look at you, look at this." She tottered backwards on her soaring suede heels, pulling Dominic's coat open. "Look at this, Mister James Bond suit, very Carnaby Street, very *very*. Beautiful. Is this Paolo's new line?"

"No, no, some shop in Yorkville, nothing special, but the tie is Cathode — can a man get a drink around here? I mean, one drink, *one drink —*"

"One drink never hurt anyone," said Danny taking his arm.

"One drink never hurt anyone, I mean, it's not as if it's every night, is it?"

Judith squealed, opening her red mouth wide to laugh and covering it with her red fingernails and arching her back so that her coat parted and revealed her black bodice, the silk tight across her belly, and her chest white and bony in the harsh light, and Danny roared and Dominic laughed despite himself, laughed helplessly, helplessly happy as they fronted the bar with its white cloth and its rows of martini glasses. The waiters in their bow ties smiled at them as they rattled their silver shakers and poured streams of clear liquid in arcs from their clear bottles.

"What do we have here?"

"Martinis, blue, green, red, what have you, with things floating. It's sponsored by —"

"Is it free?"

"Can I get just a plain one?"

"It's sponsored by Smirnoff, so of course it's free, it's more than free, they *want* you to drink it and pose for this gentleman with the camera while drinking it, and canapés, over there, from Crepuscule."

"Really? *Crepuscule?* Holy hand grenades, Batman, Crepuscule, how much did they shell out for *that* little —"

"Who's cooking there now?"

"Do they have satay? I've been craving satay all —"

"*Really?* That's so weird, because with me it's been those little baked oysters that Ritchie did at Uranium, you know, with the sesame crust? All day, *all day.*"

"Does it have to be vodka? That's not really a martini, if it's vodka."

"That's the way with these Smirnoff fellows, they won't let you have a gin martini, they're funny that way."

"Bastards. Can't a man get a drink around here?"

"Just one —"

"It's not as if it's —"

"*Just one drink!*"

"EVERY DAY!" Dominic and Danny shouted together.

The bartender was laughing with them as he shook and stirred and poured flashing drinks into tall triangular glasses. Everything around them seemed to be made of ice. They moved away, spilling drops of ice, into the cavernous open space, and looked around. The doors were officially open now, the crowd swelling in and passing up and down the rows of chairs, bending to read the name tags. The concrete around the runways was already crowded with photographers.

"Freezing cold."

"Where do the models change?"

"I think in that big truck outside."

"I hope there are no bathing suits, for their sakes."

"There's Amanda." Dominic waved. She was with a tall black man with a shaved head and a narrow navy suit that looked like at least a Paul Smith if not an actual Prada. Dominic noticed that Judith said nothing, and that Amanda did not approach them. "Are you guys still friends, since she got the job at *Edge?*"

"Well," said Judith after a tiny pause, "it's a little weird."

"I'm sorry to hear that. You guys were so close. Didn't you collaborate on the *Toronto Panty Guide?*"

"Yes, we did. For two years."

"Congratulations on that, by the way. Looks great. That's a lot of panties you guys tried on. I saw it in Chapters."

"Thank you."

"How is it selling?"

"So what are you working on, these days?" said Judith.

"Well, I just finished directing a video for Steel Box —"

"Great."

"Great. How much do you get paid for that?"

"— and I'm still trying to sell my series, you know, we have the development money for a pilot, and I'm meeting with —"

"Who's the tall guy with Amanda?" said Danny.

Judith tossed the hair from her eyes. "That's Clarence G. Purvis, the veterinarian."

"The veterinarian?"

"He's the hip vet. He's everywhere."

"The hip *vet?*" said Dominic, reaching into his breast pocket for his notebook and pen. He stopped his hand and let it drop. "And, anyway, I'm also doing some magazine writing, you know, just for money —"

"Whoring," said Danny, "but honest whoring."

"Exactly, I'd rather be working on this little short I'm writing, for —"

"How much do you think a veterinarian makes?" said Judith.

"Hey!" said Danny, poking Dominic with a surprisingly stout forefinger, "saw your piece in *Buzzer.*"

"In *Buzzer?*" said Dominic, with a twitch. "Oh, the one on —"

"You're writing for *Buzzer?*" said Judith.

"Just did a little food piece. On the new mozzarellas."

"The new mozzarellas?" Judith frowned.

"Oh, they're everywhere. It's this whole big thing. There's a new technique," Danny explained, "in making mozzarellas, over in Italy. Now everyone's serving them, it turns out we never really knew what mozzarella was until —"

"Until everyone started writing about it," said Dominic.

Judith was fumbling in her handbag. "Is everyone writing about it? Have you covered it, Danny?" She extracted a notebook and pen and began scribbling.

"We were going to, until we saw Dom's piece. Tell me, Dom, how much did they pay you for that?"

Dominic coughed. "I don't think *Edge* has covered it," he said to Judith, "if that's what you're wondering."

"Do you do a lot of work for *Buzzer?*" asked Judith.

"Oh no," said Dominic quickly. "No no. I'm really not trying to make a living at this. I'm more of a filmmaker, as you know."

"So you're not Rudix Posure, or whoever writes Dish?"

Dominic laughed. "Don't be silly."

"Do you know who it is?"

"No idea. I don't work in the office, you know."

"Well whoever it is is a true prick. You tell him from me, if you find out."

"What did he — what did they write about you?"

"Bony temptress, blah blah, always well-refreshed and universally loathed fashion editor, queen of the superficial, blah blah."

"Nasty," muttered Dominic.

"Yes, very. And then there was a story about me having my

assistant pick out the peanuts from my pad thai, completely ridiculous, completely untrue."

"Was it?" said Dominic.

"Oh, totally. Well, only half true, anyway. She volunteered to do it, Dominic, she *volunteered*, it's not as if I'm some sort of ogre forcing people to —"

"That's a strange name," said Danny, "Rudix Posure. Do you think it's a, what do you call it, a fake name?"

Judith snorted, splashing beads of vodka onto her neck and dress, where they winked for a second like diamonds before melting into shadows on the black silk. "Well *duh!* Does it sound like a real name to you?"

"A pseudonym," said Dominic quietly.

"Danny," said Judith too loudly, "it's a *joke*, don't you get it, Rudix Posure, rude, exposure, get it?"

"I've always wondered if it was just a coincidence," said Danny, blushing. Then he shrieked, "*Muriella!*" and broke from them, almost at a run, towards a middle-aged lady with very red hair. They embraced and Dominic noted that she wore a very fine coat of shiny black Merino wool and heavy round glasses and much makeup.

"Is that Muriella —?"

"Muriella *Pent*," said Judith plosively, and gulped at her martini, her eyes narrowed and gleaming.

"She's like the big socialite, right, organizes balls and lives in Wychwood Park and wants to, like *support the arts?*"

Judith snorted and Dominic laughed. "*Support the arts!*" she snorted.

They both giggled wrenchingly for a few seconds.

"She has this idea that the arts means like *ballet* —"

"And nice abstract paintings to go over the ottoman."

"*Exactly!* She wants to open her house up to hold an artist in residence or something, and if she had any idea what living with a real painter is like . . ."

Dominic watched Muriella Pent, her long black skirt and her pointy boots, and wondered about the inside of her house, and how he could apply for her program. Then he thought, for some reason, perhaps because the slit in Muriella Pent's skirt was so high and afforded a glimpse of gleaming black thigh that looked surprisingly firm and narrow for someone who lived in Wychwood Park, for some reason he thought of Leyalla.

"Oh, Judith," he said, "there's something I wanted to ask you about. I was wondering if you hire the stylists for the shoots in —"

"Do you know Danny very well?" she interrupted startlingly, leaning forward in a cloud of booze-breath, perhaps even somewhat unsteadily already.

"I — no, no I don't." Dominic took in a mouthful of vodka and regretted it. He held it there, burning his tongue and palate.

"Have you heard any rumours about him?"

Dominic shook his head. Then swallowed. Gasping, he brought out, "What kind of rumours?" His eyes were watering.

"Well, sexual preference kind of rumours."

"Really?" Dominic stared blinkingly across the rows of chairs to Danny Fineman, who had now approached Amanda Crisp and the hip veterinarian and was shaking the man's hand heartily. "Really? Danny? I don't, I wouldn't think so. Not to look at him, anyway. Why? What have you heard?"

Judith brought a red-clawed hand in front of her face for a

second, possibly to hide a demure burp, which filled Dominic with a quick gust of something like sympathy. She was looking beyond her thirty-five years for the moment. "Excuse me. I've heard that he was seen at La Pantera Rosa."

"Oh, hell," said Dominic, "*I've* been there, that doesn't mean —"

"Not smooching with a Latino boy toy in a booth in the corner you haven't."

Dominic felt his eyes widening. "Really? You heard that? From someone who was there?"

She nodded.

Again Dominic had to stop his hand from sneaking into his notebook pocket. He just had to try to remember. "Well," he said nonchalantly, "you just never know, do you? Listen, I was going to tell you, if you're ever looking for a stylist, I have a good one to recommend to you."

Judith looked at him directly for the first time that evening, her eyes sombre. "Is it Leyalla Brown?"

Dominic laughed. "Yes, yes it is. I would love you to have a look at her book, she's done a little work for *Buzzer*, and she's probably going to do something for —"

"Are you seeing her?" Judith's eyes seemed to have narrowed a little.

"Well, I guess so. In a way, yes." Dominic finished his martini, tipped the glass high to get the last drop. He felt his face heating up.

"She *is* beautiful, isn't she?" Judith was still staring at him earnestly.

"Yes." His face was really hot now. He couldn't help smiling. "Yes she is. Very."

"I mean really beautiful, genuinely beautiful. She is, Dominic."

"I know she is."

"I hope you do. I hope you realize that."

Dominic dropped his smile. "Yes, I do. I'm all too well aware of it."

"Anyway, I'd be happy to look at her book. I've been meaning to, anyway."

"Really?"

"Sure. Tell her to call me tomorrow."

"Excellent." Dominic beamed. "Thanks, Judith. She'll be — I will. Anyway. Shall we get some more of these?"

After the crush of the bar, Dominic found himself alone in a less-crowded section of concrete. He sat on a chair at the very end of a row, in the shadow of the overcurving wall, choosing a chair marked "Don Smales, *Next*," because he knew that Don Smales would not be there because Don Smales did not cover fashion and furthermore would be incapable of leaving his bar on the Danforth beyond about six o'clock on a Tuesday night, and furthermore because Don Smales, whether Don himself knew it or not — and Dominic did know it — had been fired from *Next* magazine that very morning. So Dominic sat in poor ugly unemployed Don Smales's vacant chair and, glancing about, took out his notebook.

He wrote frantically and in tiny letters:

Fashion chatterati gather in deep-freeze salt storage locker to suffer for their sins at hyperhip Mineral Ray show. Haute femmes Gall and Crisp, formerly giggly collaborators on notorious lead balloon Panty Guide *(the stone that sank new-style vanity press Snype House) seen snubbing each other — are they now at each other's throats instead of at their long suffering staff's? Who got the blame for the lead balloon book, anyway?*

He paused, looking around him. He could fix up the writing later. The idea was there. Now he was surrounded by Ryerson fashion students in platform boots, who provided sufficient cover. They were all upset at being seated so far away from the runway; two girls were standing over one chair, each with one hand on the back.

"It says here, Conceptor Representative one, two and three, and there are only two of you, so all I'm saying is —"

"All *I'm* saying, Jennifer, is that I was given three seats and I'm going to *take* three seats."

He went back to writing.

A certain hitherto apparently heterosexual fashion editor from the Daily Consterner . . .

He crossed out "fashion editor."

editor of generally feminine subject matter at otherwise unimpeachably dull Daily Consterner *seen making very close business contacts with Latino boy toy* . . .

He stopped, looked up, waved across the room at Vibica Ashe again, hiding his notebook under his coat, waited till she had vanished and took it out again. He crossed out "boy toy" — that was Judith's.

young slender gentleman of romantic Iberian origins with an apparent serious interest in rhumba, at notorious haunt of uninhibited switch-hitters . . .

He tapped the pen on the paper, crossed out "switch-hitters."

haunt of learned gendernauts everywhere.

He couldn't suppress a smile. "Gendernaut" was good. Even if he hadn't invented it himself. It was still more modern — "switch-hitter" was a little rednecky.

He saw Danny approaching from afar, Danny already red-faced, a martini in each hand, and he rose, stuffing the notebook away.

"Thought you might be thirsty," said Danny.

"Very gentlemanly, sir. Very —"

"Very *very*," said Danny. "Cheers."

"Think this will get going really late?"

"They always do. More time to ogle. And there's lots to ogle here." Danny nudged Dominic as a tall girl with orange hair slunk past on her platform boots.

"Indeed," said Dominic. "Much that is ogleable. I've always wondered if that's why you're in this business."

"Well, it's a bonus, that's for sure."

Dominic smiled and sipped. He had never heard Danny being ribald about girls before. You had to admit, it was a little suspicious. "How do you justify ogling? Aren't you a married man, so to speak? How's that beautiful girlfriend of yours?"

"Oh." Danny shrugged, scanning the rows of chairs, black hats, the massed photographers. "That didn't work out."

"Really? Are you still —?"

"Not really. It's pretty well over."

"That's too bad." Dominic watched him, his smoothly shaven face, the shiny shoes, the meticulous cuffs. There was, indeed, perhaps a hint, just a hint of delicacy in the way he had his hand on his hip.

Danny shrugged. "Not really." He turned to grin at Dominic. "Means freedom at things like these."

"Good for you."

"What about you?" said Danny. "Is it true what I hear abut you?"

"What do you hear about me?"

"About you and that incredible stylist?"

Dominic grinned back. "It depends on what you've heard."

"Come on, you know what I've heard. That you're more than friends with that incredible babe with the weird name."

"Leyalla. Leyalla Brown. Yes, we've been kind of —"

"Doing it. Sinkin' the pink."

"Danny, really, sometimes you talk like a —"

"Bonk city. Bonk-o-rama. Good for you. I mean seriously, congratulations. She is incredible."

Dominic laughed, blushing again. "I don't know quite how to take that."

"Well, I'm amazed. I don't know how you did it, but I'd like to know. If I ever slept with a woman like that I'd want to die. Seriously. There would be nothing left in your life, everything would be a let-down after that, it would be like, I would like self-immolate or something. I'd write a poem and then I'd just die. I'd die of beauty. I'd die of babeness. Cheers."

Dominic clinked his glass but did not feel quite as pleased as he knew he should. It made him feel strangely guilty, as if he were an impostor and not going out with Leyalla at all. Sometimes, indeed, he had to remind himself that he was. He had seen very little of her lately. He said, apropos of nothing, "If everything works out."

"What? You think it might not?"

Dominic shrugged. "One never knows."

"Tell me about it." Danny sipped his martini. "In fact, one knows it almost never does work out, does it?" He was not smiling.

Dominic sensed that Danny was admitting something or wanting to, a vulnerability. He wiggled his numb toes in his shoes, pulled his coat tighter around him. "Doesn't it?"

Danny didn't answer. Dominic saw the tiny opening like a distant light, a possibility of weakness and mutual confession, and he moved blindly towards it. "The problem I have," said Dominic, "is words. I talk too much."

"She not into that?"

"She's a *stylist*."

Danny nodded.

"And . . ." Dominic hesitated. He didn't really know Danny all that well. He drew a breath and said, "And I talk, I talk a lot about emotions. I'm pretty emotional and I guess she's not used to that."

"Are you?" Danny stared at him. "I wouldn't have known."

"No. But I am." He sipped at the vodka which he hated. "Now you know."

"That's okay, Dom." Danny put a hand on his shoulder. "I didn't know that. That's kind of cool."

"It's not a great thing, really. It freaks women out."

Danny nodded judiciously. "You know, sounds as if you have a power thing going here, a power imbalance. Which always happens when somebody's really beautiful and the other person, I mean not that you're not, Dom, no offence —"

Dominic let out a burst of something powerful like laughter. "No, no offence taken. Go on."

"People like that, they're really, you know, you have to say it, they're different. They have a very weird relationship to the world, and they, they don't like people who, I don't know what I'm trying to —"

"They don't like it when people like them too much because they're beautiful," said Dominic shortly.

"Is that it? I guess so. I guess that's it."

"Anyway," said Dominic, moving slightly backwards. Having tasted the faint heat of an intimate conversation, he wanted to back away from it before it burned him. "Anyway, if it doesn't work out, it doesn't."

"Cheers."

"Cheers. This is horrible stuff, by the way."

Danny nodded. "Mine is getting warm."

"Mine isn't. Mine is freezing cold. Everything is freezing cold. When do you think it's going to *start?*" Dominic remembered, suddenly, what he was going to do to Danny, as Dish, and felt a slight niggling worry that it might not be a nice thing to do, since it was turning out that he might quite like Danny and that he might not be gay after all. But there was nothing he could do, he realized quickly; Dish was just work. Work was work and Dish was not him, himself, really. Nobody knew it was him, so it wasn't him. Besides, Dish was something impersonal, something someone had to write, and if he didn't, someone else would; it was something that was going to happen to all of them and there was nothing anyone could do about it.

It was there that he had a sudden image of Christine, whom he hadn't seen for two years, and it burned his belly like something he had swallowed. He had no idea why.

He looked up at the underside of the great domed roof of the salt hangar and felt lonely. He wished the thing would start because he wanted to get home and see Leyalla, maybe have a talk about everything that had been going on or hadn't been going on, and not take all night about it because he had to be up early in the morning to write this damn thing up.

Thinking of work reminded him of something else. "By the way, Danny, have you ever seen her book, I mean Leyalla's book? She's quite good, you know, she's worked editorial shoots for *Buzzer* and *Stun* and, I mean, I don't want to tell you who to use, but if you ever need a — "

"Is she? Well, send her over. I'd love to use her." Danny pushed his face too close to Dominic's. "That is, if you trust me."

"Oh, I trust you," said Dominic confidently, finishing his drink of burning ice made of frozen gasoline, "I trust you all right."

Danny led him through the crowd and up onto one runway to cross it — there was a heady second of standing at the very intersection of the runways where the spotlights were brightest and being dazzled, when they lost their direction and stood there for a second stunned, rotating in the light, as rows of faces flashed towards them, turning to see who they were, and then turned away again, disappointed, before they clambered down again — across to the side of the room in the wash of cold from the great gaping truck entrance doors where the security men stood, still unbelievably filtering a queue outside, scrutinizing the proffered salt shakers with their long, black flashlights, parting and then closing again. There were Amanda and the slim black veterinarian in his Prada suit, and a swaying assistant editor with the shock of white hair, whose name Dominic could never remember, and whom he had never, he realized, seen sober.

"Dominic," said Amanda, "sweetie, *mwa*, how *are* you? You remember Alexina —"

"Alexina, nice to —"

"Dominic," muttered the white-haired woman, leaning forwards and almost missing his face; his nose brushed her neck.

"And have you met Clarence, Clarence G. Purvis, Dominic, Dominic's one of our up-and-coming new director types, his short film was almost nominated for a Genie."

"Good to meet you, man." The hip veterinarian's smile was wide, his handshake strong. His suit was really beautiful.

A vast tray of canapés passed; Dominic lunged and grabbed two cones of tuna tartare on crispy potato lattices. "Gotta love Crepuscule," he said, munching.

"Dominic," muttered Alexina in his ear. "Look at me. Is my lipstick okay?"

"Sure," he murmured back. He wiped his mouth. "It's fine."

She was holding on to his arm, breathing cigarettes into his ear. "Jeez, I'm loaded. I am so loaded."

"It's fine."

"No, really, tell me, because I did it without a mirror. Tell me if it's all wonky."

"Really. It's fine."

"I am so *loaded.*"

"So Dominic," said Clarence G. Purvis, "do you write about fashion too?"

"Not really," said Dominic. "I just go where there's free booze. Do you?"

"Same thing, man. Same thing." They both laughed and Dominic decided he liked Clarence G. Purvis.

"Maybe I should eat something," said Alexina.

"When do you think this thing is going to start?"

"Who wants another drink?"

When the lights finally went down and the music reared up, hard and hysterical, Dominic was between Danny and Judith, right against the runway. The photographers were kneeling at their feet, which was sort of awkward, and Dominic knew that once the models came out they would all stand in front of him so he would have to stand and everyone behind him would have to stand, too. The lights went down, spotlights danced on the runway, a white glow came up behind the screen they had put in front of the truck doors, the first two models emerged from behind it, stalking and angry, the beat hammered, the electric guitars screamed and echoed in the dome, and Dominic felt his heart pounding faster and his face flushing; he stood up with the entire front row as the photographers stood up.

Helplessly, he grinned as the first model loomed over him on heels like steeples, all bones, swished past him; he was so close he could see the goose bumps on her bare back, the red lines where her bra had been; he could smell her toxic hairspray, see the little pocks on the plexiglass runway imprinted by her spike heels; she passed, flapping fabric and showering him with a trail of glamour like sparks. Then there was another one and another and another, in silks and spandex and diaphanous lace; there were nipples and more goose flesh, velvet ribbons and bony ankles, bare arms going mottled in the cold. One wore a skirt so short Dominic looked up it and saw a flash of white thong between tiny little buttocks.

"Some bonkable chicks, man," said Danny.

The women along the runways in their black coats watched and shivered and made notes with hard faces.

"I love it," Danny was saying, "I love it. I'm so happy."

There were muscular, hairless, oily boys in white underwear and tans accompanying the next set, evening gowns: the boys were held on leashes by the women in long, flared skirts that clung like shiny film, their hair piled up into points; they looked like communications towers.

"I like the super tall one," said Danny. "She has a little more flesh on her, at least. She's bonkable."

The photographers in front of them began to jostle, as James Bond theme music started up, and two stunt men in dinner jackets came out, pursued by Ninja warriors in black pyjamas. There was some convincing stage-fighting: the James Bond men succeeded in flipping the warriors gracefully. This was a prelude to a bikini segment with girls in gold body paint and dyed gold hair.

"It's a *Goldfinger* thing, I guess," said Danny. "Highly bonkable. Eminently bonkable."

Dominic realized that his teeth were chattering in the cold and that he had to pee. He wondered what if anything anyone would do if one of the models collapsed with hypothermia.

There was an English romantic nineteenth-century thing with Empire dresses, except that they were all diaphanous, shifting sheets of lace and mesh and the vague shadows of nipples and pubic hair.

"Yikes," said Dominic, moved. "That's too sexy."

"Bonk-o-rama," yelped Danny. "Bonk*eration!*"

Dominic decided for sure that Danny was gay.

There was a lot of milling about afterwards as people decided on alliances and migrations. Dominic stood for a few minutes in a shadow with his back to the crowd, writing in his notebook:

> — *cold provided plethora of nipples.*
> — *everybody saying very very. Something about new verbal tic of inarticulately cool.*
> — *who is Vibica with?*
> — *would-be artiste Muriella Pent finds herself far from leafy Wychwood, having taken wrong turn at Chanel boutique on Bloor Street.*

Then he wandered, and found himself with Danny and Amanda and white-haired Alexina and Clarence G. Purvis, Judith Gall having noticeably left in a hurry, alone. "I could use some dinner," said Clarence G. Purvis.

"Umberto's," said Dominic.

"Fine," said Purvis. "I have a car."

"Excellent," said Dominic. He really liked Clarence G. Purvis.

The veterinarian greeted a number of people as they entered Umberto's, including the new red-haired waitress whom Dominic had never had the courage to speak to, and Umberto himself, who stood at the head of the line of people waiting for tables as if barring entrance to the dining room.

They shook hands with big smiles. Umberto seemed to already have five menus in his hand; he led the way towards a booth. Dominic had the impression of floating through the tables. It seemed extraordinarily dim and dinny.

"Do you know that waitress's name?" said Danny, once they were seated.

Clarence G. Purvis smiled. "No. I can't remember."

"Man," said Danny, his head in his hands as if mourning, "I can't believe her. Bonk-o-licious."

"I can't really afford anything but pasta," said Dominic to himself.

"Have anything you want," said the veterinarian softly. "It's on me. Does anyone know anything about where to go in London? I'm going tomorrow."

"London England?"

"Yeah. You know, where to go, where people are going now."

"No idea," said Dominic gloomily. "I never go anywhere."

"Hey," said Danny, "I saw your house in *House and Home*, I mean your loft or your condo or whatever it is."

"My space," said Purvis, smiling. He shrugged.

"It's beautiful. Incredibly beautiful," said Danny in the same tone of deep sadness. "It's the most beautiful thing I've ever seen in there."

"Your space was in *House and Home?*"

"It's the most beautiful thing," said Amanda, turning her thin face up to the halogen light, "I've ever seen in my life."

"Cool," said Dominic. "Who designed it?"

"Kazimoto Stockwell."

"Really? Wow. Wow." Dominic closed his eyes and pictured Clarence G. Purvis's space, a surgical cathedral of vast white walls, all stainless steel and green glass, catwalks and galleries high above, bathrooms like swimming pools. He pictured the bedroom like a Japanese clothing store, with all the clothes black and grey and charcoal. He pictured it like a national art gallery.

"And Andy Nottingham took the pictures," said Amanda.

"Really? I thought he was in New York now."

"He is," said Purvis. "He came up just to shoot my space."

"Do you mind," said Dominic, "if I have the rack of lamb?"

Alexina squeezed his thigh under the table. She put her nose into his ear and said, "Where are we, exactly?"

"Is everybody ready to order?" said the red-haired waitress.

Danny smiled up at her, humming a little song. "Bonk-a-*di*lly, bonk-a-*de*lic, bonk-a-*roo*-ney-*oo*ney."

"Well," said Dominic to Danny and Alexina, "that was nice of him." They were standing on the street outside Umberto's and wondering whether to button up their coats. The veterinarian had shaken all their hands powerfully and even kissed Alexina on her powdery cheek and then taken Amanda away in his car. Now they were just holding their coats together in the wind, in case another black car suddenly appeared and opened its doors to take them somewhere else.

Danny and Alexina snorted simultaneously. "He's all right," said Danny, "if you don't mind all the bullshit."

"What bullshit?"

"*House and Home*," blurted Alexina, "I'll pay for everything, la-di-da —"

"But he was in *House and Home*, wasn't he? You saw it, right?"

"Yeah, but —"

"But what? You did let him pay for your dinner, didn't you?"

"Well," said Danny, finally buttoning his coat, "did you see the way he had his hand on Amanda's shoulder as they left? It was gross."

Dominic laughed. "Oh, I see. Gross. Disgusting."

"Well, it's not gross, it's just I didn't expect it, that's all. She's my friend and I didn't know anything about it." He sounded a little whiny.

Dominic shivered.

"Where are we going now?" said Alexina, lighting a cigarette.

"I'm on my way home." Dominic stepped into the street to look for a cab.

"Does anyone want to come to my place for a drink?" said Alexina, looking at Dominic.

"No, thanks. Goodnight, everyone. Goodnight."

Dominic let them have the first cab that came, then waited until they were out of sight, and walked to a payphone on the corner. He dialled his own number. Leyalla did not answer. He heard his own message and said, "Hello hello hello hello hello hello hello hello," into the machine but she did not pick up, so he said, "Okay, I guess you're not there. You must be on your way over. If you are there, it's me and I'm on my way home now, and you'll be pleased because I have some really good news, you'll be really pleased with me. I talked you up to everybody and they all suddenly love you and they want to see your book. You've got work for six months out of this, I bet. I promise. You'll be happy. And it was really good for me, too, I got great stuff for Dish, really great stuff. Trini will freak. She'll be ecstatic. About Danny and Judith and Amanda and all of them. I'll tell you all about it, I can't wait. Okay. See you in a few minutes, then."

He hung up. He hesitated before leaving the phone booth. He didn't know why, but he had an urge to call his machine again and listen to his messages before he got home. It was silly, since he would be home in ten minutes, in a second really.

In the cab he closed his eyes and pictured the tight curls of Leyalla's hair, the copper skin of her neck. His head was full of lace and bare thighs; he realized he was excited. He let his mind slip down between her breasts, felt his heart accelerate. He opened his eyes and leaned forward, slapping his hand on his thigh. He wanted to see her.

His studio was dark. It smelled of the cigarettes of the people downstairs. They seemed to have been smoking all day.

He looked around, as he took off his coat, for traces of Leyalla but found none. He turned on some lamps. She had not been there. The apartment seemed small.

He went to the ancient answering machine on his desk and hesitated for a second before pressing the flashing button. There were just two new messages, meaning the one he had left and one other. He sat down and turned the lamp on and took a deep breath and pressed it.

She said, very quickly, "Hi, it's me, I'm sorry, I'm not coming over, I don't think it's a good idea. I'm going to be out for a while and . . ." There was a long pause. There was traffic noise behind her voice. "I don't think I'll see you for a while, Dominic. I don't think we should see each other every day. It's not right for me and I'm just not . . . I don't know. I'm sorry. Anyway. Sorry. Bye."

Dominic sat for a while at the desk. He rose and got a glass of murky water from the tap. Then he went to his coat where it hung on the wall and fished in the pockets until he found the hard-edged salt shaker. He took it out and put it on the windowsill where there was already an orange silk handkerchief printed with florid script, a gold soup can with letters punched in the side in tiny holes, and an origami swan which had once contained a sachet of a new perfume whose scent Dominic could not recall.

LIONEL

Desire

The brick is red-yellow, burned or burnished. If a rough surface could appear polished, this is what it would look like; the brick is lambent (if a flame were motionless, somehow distilled into a colour of flameness, static lambency). The brick is part of a wall, part of a high office or condominium building on Bay Street. Lionel is looking up at it, at the high warm brick in the late afternoon sun. It is this colour, of course, because of the sun, and the time of day when the sun is so low it turns to stage lighting, a row of gas footlights on the horizon. The sky behind and above the building is blue, a completely artificial blue.

The day is even hot, unusually hot for so far into the fall, and people are at once elated and disconcerted by it: men are already wearing dark wool suits, and they must loosen their ties as they walk a few blocks before glancing at their watches and surrendering to the subway. They are walking slowly, experiencing confusing sensory stimulations and memories of previous summers, including this past summer, already consigned to photo albums, superimposed in a too-rapid edit.

There is a park with trees with leaves like butter flecked with green herbs, perhaps with tarragon.

There are a few people sitting at tables outside a restaurant. There is a woman in a business suit, waiting for someone. She is blonde, and as she leans over her menu her silk blouse flutters slightly in the wind that rushes up and down this street all day, a wind that always makes this particular terrace, on a canyon of a street, impractical (which is disappointing, because the wicker chairs are so pretty). She does not seem to mind the wind; she leans into it and closes her eyes. Her blouse opens slightly, too quickly to reveal flesh or lace strap, and closes again. The fabric of her shirt is flimsy, barely opaque.

On a sidestreet running between Bay and University there is another expensive condominium building set slightly back from the street, with a newly built, curving driveway made of interlocking L-shaped bricks. This brick is darker, potting-soil-toned. The sun is so low it makes fine lines of shadow between each tessellated brick. There are concrete posts, meant to look like stone, flanking the entrance to the driveway, the kind of small towers or cairns that flank driveways to country estates, topped with stone balls, and which have a name which Lionel can't recall, something beginning with *p*, like postern or postilion or pillion, but none of those; these posts, for want of an accurate word (*post* connotes *wood*, which is unsatisfying), are crowned instead with four-sided glass lanterns containing real burning gas flames. It is funny, he thinks, that he was just thinking of gas footlights. The lobby of the building, glimpsable through a glass wall, is creamily modern and spotless. The whole building and wastefully ornate and immaculately new mosaic driveway arrangement is almost European in its luxury, it is bright as the sky.

In the hot crowd on Yonge Street, there are clusters of Mediterranean girls, walking so fast they are almost running, giggling and tangled together, in tight cotton tops with thin straps and bare shoulders. Not one of them is wearing a bra. Their nipples are bumps. In the window of the big Le Chateau store are mannequins wearing miniskirts and sparkly tights. He goes into the loud bass music and notes that this is where the tight tops with thin straps come from, and fingers the sparkly tights, which are scratchy. There are also opaque grey ones, dove grey. He is also glancing at a salesgirl behind the counter who is also wearing one of the cotton tops; her breasts are bigger than most and swaying, and the cotton is so thin her nipples are visible not just as bumps, but as entire aureoles, almost unbelievably beautiful, with two surfaces in relief, the wider disks showing their edges as tiny ridges. Indeed, there is even a faint colour visible through the white cotton, the circles of aureole perceptible as darker regions like craters on an image of a planet blurred by distance.

He talks with her about Sandra's height and weight (rather proudly; he likes shaking his head over the medium, oh no, much too big), and buys the riskier, scratchier sparkly ones from her.

He stops at Umberto's on College Street on the way home, for a drink at the bar which smells of coffee and beer and cologne and French cigarettes; the day is still too bright for reentering domesticity. He orders a manhattan in a large martini glass. There is a dark girl sitting next to him, no older than twenty, who must be a Catholic, for she wears a silver cross tightly to her neck. Her blouse is open low. The skin beneath the cross is coffee-coloured. His manhattan arrives, a tower of a drink, the glass frosty, the rust-coloured liquid misty with crushed ice. Mariella has sculpted such a long twist of lemon rind it curls in coils inside the glass, over-flowing one edge like a tentacle. The drink is cold and sweet and cinnamony and bitter from the lemon rind. Someone down the bar is smoking a cigar.

By the time he reaches his front door and fumbles with the key the air is blue and cool; it will be suddenly cold. Sandra is home, cooking something in wine. She barely turns to look at him as he enters. Her shoulders are hunched over the stove. He kisses the back of her neck and she does not respond. He turns her to face him and he sees that she is frowning, her eyes distant. He says, "Are you okay?"

She says, "Uh-huh. I'm fine."

With a gentle thumb, he smooths the lines between her eye-brows. "What's the matter?"

"Nothing." She buries her head on his shoulder. She squeezes him.

He kisses her neck and then her mouth, wetly.

She says, "What's with you?" and smiles a little. She plays with his hair. She is surprised.

He pulls the elastic from her hair and shakes it free. Still she seems distracted. He can't stop kissing her neck, which makes her wriggle. He smacks her bum. She says, "Ow!" and sticks her tongue in his mouth; it tastes of wine.

They are on the couch and he has his hand between her thighs in the scratchy, sparkly tights. She says, "I like them." She points both toes into the air, ignoring his hand and its insistent pressure, swinging her knees to one side and then the other, her head canted to view her thighs in the light. "I *love* them."

"Good for flitting in."

"Flit flit."

"Do some flitting," he says. "Show me some flitting. Just a little flit."

She rises, and in her T-shirt and tights runs in little steps, on the balls of her feet, from one end of the living room to the other, with her hands outstretched behind her, her head tossing from side to side, a mock frightened expression on her face. "*Flitting*," she chants, "*flitting!*"

He is clapping his hands and laughing. "Flit, flit!"

She leaps over the coffee table, so light, and back, flits into the kitchen.

"Ballet dancer leaving the stage!" he shouts.

She pauses, composes herself (he can see her through the arch between kitchen and living room, under the harsh kitchen light), places her glittering legs together in first position, brings her arched fingers together at her crotch, her elbows flexed, and with her chest rising and falling from the last dance, she smiles at the audience and curtsies deeply, pulling her hands wide apart as if lifting her skirt. She then widens her arms, looks to the ballerinas to her left and right, smiling widely, encouraging them to step forward, to take her hands; her hands joined with theirs, she bows deeply. As he continues clapping and whistling and calling "*Bis*," she bows again and then turns — and this is the climax, his moment of delight — holding her invisible skirt with dainty forefinger and thumb, flits with tiny steps off the stage, down the corridor to the bedroom.

He follows her, applauding, to the dim bedroom, where she is stripping off her tights and T-shirt. He falls on the bed to watch her. Once naked, she does not join him, but flits out into the dark corridor. He follows her into the now dark living room, as even the twilight has vanished with a wintery suddenness, where she is flitting in shadow, her pale skin a faint glow, a cold light with a dark smudge, a buzz at its centre. She even flits brazenly out into the brightness of the kitchen where the windows are uncurtained and the light of the interior, containing her image, broadcast out onto the dark wall and windows of the neighbouring building. She flits back into the living room and falls on him, on the couch, where he kisses her breasts and neck and holds her waist between finger and thumb, testing its narrowness. He places her on the couch, slips to the floor and nuzzles his nose between her legs, into the darkness, fuzz and earth. She lifts her calves to his shoulders. He licks her there and gently probes her with his tongue, tasting the salty sweet and tart, and she bunches his hair in her tight fingers, her back arching, saying "Oh."

He rises the length of her body to kiss her lips so that she can taste herself on him and to press himself against her, for he now has a deep thirst for friction, and he says to her, as he often says, barely conscious of repeating himself, "You're so small," which always embarrasses her. "You're so small," he says, as he kisses her. "You're little."

"No," she says.

"I'll protect you."

She goes quiet at this and perhaps even stiffens slightly, but it is probably nothing. He says, "Let me get a condom."

She sighs as if she doesn't want him to.

He strokes her face and tries to smile and says, "No little babies."

And now she is completely still. She says, "Don't say that."

"Don't say what?"

"You know what."

He is still for a second. "I'm not even allowed to *say* babies now?"

"Do you need to say it, that same thing every time? Just to remind me?"

He sighs. He sits up on the couch. "Why not?"

She is silent for a long time and when she speaks her voice is thin. "Babies. Don't keep saying it. I hate it when you say that."

"Sorry." He gets up and moves towards the bedroom to get the condom but he feels suddenly heavy. He turns to look at her, a white vagueness against the dark couch, a gap among the shadows, and he feels a spark of anger and he says, "Why now? Why right now do you have to bring that up again?"

"Me bring it up again? You were the one who said it."

He bites his lip. "And every time I so much as *mention* . . . I mean, *Christ.* Haven't we been through this enough?"

She is crying. "No," she says finally. "No we haven't."

He sits with her on the couch. He puts his arm around her. They sit for five minutes, maybe ten. It's all over now. Now it's just a question of talking and apologizing and trying to contain his anger. He wonders if the hockey game has begun. He wants to either throw her on her back or get up and watch the game.

She is sobbing. "I've been feeling it all day," she says between sobs. "I'm sorry."

He says nothing. The room is almost black now. He strokes her hair. "Why?" he says. "Why now?"

She sobs louder. "Why not?" she wails. She bunches her fist

and brings it down in a meaty slap against his arm. "I don't get it. I don't *get* it. *Why* not?"

He jerks his hand away. A fatigue comes down on him like sand. He sighs. He can't explain, to her, again, how it seems like a rejection of him, how he thought she wanted him, his real tongue and stubbly chin and distended cock and ugly balls, him, and sees suddenly sometimes that she wants something else, something much bigger and more powerful and more important to her than him, mere him.

He looks at her, her little breasts white shadows moving faintly. He can't imagine why she wants to end her own youth. And if they talk about it now, again, even that will be giving in to it. He says softly, "Every time now, sweetie. Every time we start to —"

"I know," she says. "I'm sorry. But I just don't understand."

He is thinking of all the things he can't explain to her, of his image of the mothers at Umberto's in the afternoons. He sees them in the afternoons, in the café part, when he is trying to work there, with his fountain pen and his string of espressos in the low light and the murky jazz, before the perfumes and cigarette smoke of the after-work crowd at the bar, he sees the mothers in their overalls and sweatshirts across the room, meeting each other for coffee, with their enormous strollers blocking the aisles, and all the bottles and blankets and wailing and shushing and no-no-no-ing. He knows some of these mothers: some of them are people he has met in television stations and publishing houses. They were young when he knew them. He doesn't see any of them any more anywhere else, except in the café part of Umberto's in the afternoons, makeupless and fat. They are all exhausted; they exhaust everyone around them. He can see them trying to talk, distracted by the wailing, the falling down, the constant menace of injury and liquid spillage, of bodily mess. It makes him bored just to look at them as they wait there, for that is all that they are doing, waiting there for the sun to go down and Daddy to come home, so that they can be waiting for him there, in a bright, hot, smelly apartment, so that they tell him what they did all day, so that they can say, "We've had *such* an interesting day, haven't we, Booboo?"

There is a frying fat smell seeping into the apartment from across the hall. It fills the apartment in half a minute. It is as if the room has suddenly grown smaller. Lionel closes his eyes and sees the caramel colour of the manhattan in its frosty glass, the coffee neck of the Catholic girl in Umberto's. The cross cool on her skin. He rises blindly, moving towards the door.

He picks his jacket up from the kitchen chair where he had draped it. He says, "I can't go on talking about this," and leaves her crying on the couch. Outside, it is freezing cold. He looks up, tries to distinguish the elaborate gable on the Victorian house opposite. He loves this gable as the sun sets, for a red glow turns it purple. But it is too dark; he can't discern any of the features of the buildings on the street.

The
Stockholm
Syndrome

■

Lionel Baratelli was a very well known author. *Very well known.*

This is what he repeated to himself on the bus from Wolfville to Yarmouth in the blizzard. He couldn't see out the windows for white. He could feel the rear wheels fishtailing every now and then with a nauseous shudder, then finding the tracks again with a thump, and he clutched the plastic armrest tighter. He fingered his neat goatee.

Had not his last novel been shortlisted for the Ontario Booksellers' Award? Had it not been reviewed in the *Village Voice Literary Supplement?* (Not well, admittedly, and only In Brief, but everyone knew that even getting *in* was a major accomplishment for a Canadian writer, and did his publisher not keep repeating gleefully, "Column inches, Li, column inches"?)

Was *Edge* magazine not about to excerpt a brilliantly minimalist passage from the new book, in their Christmas issue, no less? Was this not his *third* book? What other writer of his age — early forties — had already published three books?

Well, Ontario writer, anyway?

What about the option on his second novel, *Glitter Dive*, that he had just sold to Pyramid Pictures, who were, his agent Michiyo assured him, 99 per cent certain they were going to spring for the rights, outright rights? This, surely, should have turned him into a grown-up. Indeed, on the strength of this assurance, Lionel had put down a payment on the very first automobile he would ever have owned, a late but unequivocal indicator, surely, of adulthood?

What the question came down to was, *What the fuck was he doing here?*

The rear of the bus veered, the wheels grinding on some sort of rough surface under the snow — gravel on the shoulder? — and Lionel pulled his overcoat blanket higher up to his chin. The bus was moving even slower now, crawling at no more than ten or twenty through the white-out. The heat seemed to have died as well. The interiors of the windows were frosting up. He looked around at his unbelievable fellow travellers, thank god almost all sleeping. The man in the opposite window seat, a large dormant slug. He had a cap attached to his skull which read "John Deere." His tongue and belly both hanging out. A half-eaten tangerine clutched in his fist. A smell of diesel oil, old underwear, warm tangerine. This guy, this guy's sleep was *unfathomably* deep; needles through his skin would probably just disappear with a sucking noise, like bullets into a harp seal. Higher life forms, Lionel reflected, could have no way of imagining such a total loss of consciousness; the molecules of each of this organism's cells had ceased vibrating, slowed to a stall, atoms and quarks in a sort of suspension as if near absolute zero. He had seen this in a science program.

Occasionally the bus's sidelights picked out a mailbox in the snow, and reflective lettering: Leblanc, Babette, Robichaud. Lionel saw three Leblancs and two Robichauds.

And then there was the talkative one, two or three seats ahead, a woman's voice which had been relentlessly entertaining some entirely silent and possibly sleeping or even non-existent neighbour with a genealogy, a genealogy of her extended family — a family which had branches in pretty well every town in the Maritime provinces and whose tangled bloodlines were apparently *spreading*, Lionel had heard to his horror, like a fantastic replication of pod people, like a deep-jungle virus, to nearly every human habitation in the known world. "Now that was my sister's little girl's husband," she would say, "and they winup to Calgary, *hyup*" — they all said "yup," Lionel had observed, with an intake of breath — "*hyup*, been gone four years now and nobody heard a word, until his other cousin, the MacDonald girl from Pubnico Landing, she was up in Thunder Bay, she married the McInnis boy who was in Forestry and they —"

None of which outdid the Walkman emissions of the long-haired youth in the team jacket behind him, a heavy-metal screeching with no discernible melody, just feedback and wails over a ticking beat only just within earshot, punctuated occasionally by a bump against the back of Lionel's seat which he assumed was the youth's bobbing head.

The error, Lionel supposed, if he had to face it square on, was in putting out a book like this one in the first place. This was his clever book, his artistic statement. No more subtly moving stories about relationships. No more inexorable divorces among academics. If he was going to be forever tarred as a queasy misanthropist by ever-younger reviewers — he would swear, would Lionel, that

they were hiring them directly out of high schools these days, rip-
ping the Nintendo sets out of their hands and handing them a
painstakingly quiet work of literature, which they would sneering-
ly read in amusement arcades and *raves* or whatever, between blasts
of crystal meth or whatever it was now, Christ, he could picture
them reading his laboriously metaphorical, simile-laden sentences
from under their dreadlocks, hitching up their flapping, dragging
trousers and settling down to triumphantly write, "Baratelli's characters, implausibly, seem blissfully unaware of the real
economic/technological/race issues that lie between them, as little
effort is made to address globalization/the Internet/the real nature
of systemic racism, and his baroquely literary language does little
to move them out of their self-obsessed middle-class world, or to
allay our suspicions of elitism" — well, he would show them. If
they wanted cold, he would give them cold. This time he had got
tough. He had excluded all emotion, all explanation. His characters, menial labourers with massive, hypertrophied, meaningless
educations, registered surfaces only; they did not think. Nor did
they feel, at least explicitly (and there, Lionel thought with mount-
ing excitement, there was where the really clever analyses will come
through). A truly urban panorama, in all its emptiness; a vast,
unconnected highway system of mall chains and fast food,
fluorescent-lit offices with nobody in them. Nor were the characters — if characters they were; voices was the word he was plan-
ning to use, in interviews, disconnected voices like those of crossed
telephonic wires, or perhaps he should say something about com-
puters? — nor were they really connected, for what in reality was?
Their proto-plots brushed against, overlapped each other like shifting planes. Reality does not condescend to plot. Reality, as seen

through a truly contemporary eye. This time, they would recognize, he had refined his skill.

Baratelli has wholeheartedly embraced the modernist experiment. He pictured with tantalizing vividness all the variations on this phrase that he could expect to see in print. The great modernist adventure. Baratelli's new formalism. Baratelli has honed his vision to a razor-like coldness. Baratelli's relentlessly external gaze.

If anyone attempted to understand what he was trying to do at all. For so far the experiment had not been a great success. Despite what the teenage reviewers wanted, the publishers only seemed to want something with a murder in it. Failing, of course, a foreign locale. Even MacRobert, the greying monolith of the national publishing industry, who had halfheartedly published his first two books — books which were, also, he was proud to say, resolutely murder-free (although his first had had an Eastern European setting, not by cynical design but because Lionel had happened to live there for three years) — even MacRobert had spoken nervously to him about his evolution as a writer demanding what they subtly called "a larger canvas," or "a heightened drama." Michiyo, his agent, had explained this to him. She had gently prodded him to include a sexual fetish; she had even, outrageously, suggested he work a murder in somewhere, or at least a crime, any crime — and he had nobly, bravely refused, stuck true to his art, ploughed on like this bus through the snow, and that, he supposed, was why the book, this "novel" (not really a novel, he had stressed to anyone who would listen; he preferred the French *récit*, narrative, for its structuralist connotations) had come out with some press he had never heard of called Loon Lake and not with MacRobert, and why there was no money for a tour to the hotels of New York and

Washington, but instead this bus trip through the university residences of Canada, and why he was en route from a half-empty lecture hall to a half-empty library room in a town where there wasn't even a community college. ("There's a teachers' college, though," his publisher Jack Thalamus of Loon Lake had assured him, "and an Acadian university, which is supposed to be pretty artsy, with a theatre program and everything, and they must have to take English some time and they must be starved for culture, right? It'll be packed!") He wished he were at least still in Halifax, where there had been a frightening but hysterically sexual basement bar where all the girls were drunk. He would have to write about that bar some time.

His eyes were closed and flickering like screens, a sort of slide show: the sign for Digby and the ferry to New Brunswick, a beach in Italy he had visited, a frightening bar he had just seen in Halifax, Sandra's naked back in the bathroom in Toronto, a teachers' college which looked like a prison in this town he was approaching.

The bus was stopped and he was cold. His mouth and eyes were sticky. He tugged his coat around him. The windows were still white, but the passengers were lined up in the aisle, stepping off into the darkness. He yanked his bag out from under the seat.

The Yarmouth bus terminal must have been built in a freak period of prosperity in the late 1940s. It was the only building on the highway, bleeding light out onto the snowy fields. The paint was now peeling and the chrome letters of the sign read "GEHO CAC LIES." Both ticket windows appeared to be closed, and there were three or four people in parkas and farm equipment caps waiting inside. Lionel waited in the cold for the bags to be unloaded, then hauled his into the fluorescence. The other passengers immediately dissipated, their welcomes having been effected in silence, and he was left looking at a little man with a beard and glasses and a denim jacket, who waved brightly and moved forwards.

"Tim Dwyer," he said, seizing the suitcase, "how you doing? Good trip? I'm the Fundy Arts Council. I'm handling your accommodation, and, everything."

Lionel followed him outside and looked around for a car.

"Now. Shouldn't be too hard to get a taxi."

"Taxi?"

"Council will pay." Tim Dwyer smiled widely. "No problem."

They stood on the side of the highway. There was still snow falling. Lionel could see no evidence of a town anywhere.

"Had a good trip?"

Lionel was at a loss for a second. "Fine, thank you."

"Now I told Reggie MacDonald to be here at around this time." Tim Dwyer was looking at his watch. "He waits around the rink after hockey — we have a very active high school team here, and all the parents and fans go, it's quite an event, you might want to check it out during your stay, I can arrange for a ticket if you like. Anyways, Reggie normally comes up with a few fares out of it, especially if the weather's bad, like today. Now where the hell *is* that man? Excuse my language."

Lionel turned up the collar on his coat. A dump truck which appeared to be full of snow rumbled past. "Where am I staying?"

"Oh, you're staying with me. Just a couch, I'm afraid, but a comfortable one, and I've got a sleeping bag and blankets all ready. We had another artist come up here last year, I arranged that too, and she stayed with me too, it was no problem."

"Another writer?"

"Oh, no, no, she did puppeteering. You may know her, she's apparently, well, this is what I hear, anyways, she's the biggest name in puppeteering in Halifax at least, which is why we brought her up here, you know Gayathri Graunstein?"

"No."

"Very, *very* sweet girl, woman I should say. Oh my *stars* did we have a good time when she was here. I'll have to take you to Passages, you'd love it there, show you some local culture, and I'd be happy to buy you a good Scotch, because I've been doing my research, and I happen to have found out you like Scotch. There are some people just dying to meet you, we're pretty starved for culture out here" — he was chuckling jerkily and shaking his head — "as you can imagine."

"Thank you," said Lionel, "but I'm awfully tired, I've been travelling a lot and —" He jumped back from the road.

"Here he is! Whoa, Reggie, you almost killed us! Get in, Lionel, do you mind if I call you Lionel?"

"After you, my good sir. Take your shoes off at the top, if you don't mind."

Lionel puffed as he carried his bag to the top of the narrow stairs. The walls were imitation-wood panelling; it smelled of cigarettes and bacon fat. The apartment's floor was grey linoleum; the walls were all the same panelling. There were a few bookshelves filled with science-fiction paperbacks. He almost fell against Tim Dwyer in the corridor as he struggled with his shoes.

They padded into a living room where the walls were green and the floor was linoleum, also green. Tim Dwyer flipped on an overhead light. Lionel sat on a corduroy couch with a disintegrating hooked rug thrown over it. He supposed he should be thankful there was a frosted glass covering over the light. Were he to write this scene, he might be tempted to turn it into a naked bulb. The rest of the apartment was up to naked-bulb standards. The smell of bacon fat was stronger in the living room.

"Now," said Tim Dwyer, sitting majestically. He produced cigarettes and matches. "Now you just make yourself comfortable." He lit a cigarette and Lionel's throat contracted. Tim Dwyer reached behind him for the bottle of Scotch and two glasses, improbably clean. "I suppose you'll be wanting to know something about me."

It took an hour before Lionel could convince him that he wanted to sleep. Tim had remembered to refill his glass only twice during this time. *During*, Lionel thought, is what is happening to this time. Time dures. This time dured one hour. During which time Lionel had learned that Tim, who must have been about five years younger than Lionel, had grown up in Yarmouth, and about Tim's year and a half in Ottawa — a period which reminded Tim *so* much of Lionel's first novel, *Jake, Blasé*, which was set in Prague, because it was such a similar experience because Tim had lived in a shared house full of artistic people too, during that time, in Ottawa, much like Lionel's hero, Jake, except that the people, the guys, were in marketing, mostly, rather than sculpture, but still he could really relate — and about the arts community in Yarmouth, which had only existed since recently, in fact since the creation of the Fundy Arts Council, an invention of the Ministry of Employment and Immigration. Tim had luckily qualified for the only full-time position this council required, having been unemployed for the requisite preceding ten months. Luckily again, there hadn't been much competition for the job, since few Yarmouthians could boast, as Tim could, of an interest in the arts. Tim was interested. He liked artists. They were different. They livened things up.

"Of course," said Tim graciously, "you'll be wanting to catch up on your rest, because you have a long day tomorrow. I suggest we get up about seven? Because I've set up a meeting for you at eight with our local member of the provincial parliament. It's kind of my mandate to show you around, get people, I mean the community, get the community aware, you know? And I'm sure she'd love to meet you."

The pillowcase and the sleeping bag had been in a closet or laundry hamper for a very long time. Lionel dozed and woke throughout the night. He dreamed Tim Dwyer had come out of his room and was looming over him with a bottle of Scotch in his hand. He dreamed of Sandra shouting at him, and when he woke up he missed Sandra.

At seven Tim Dwyer was standing over him. He was going to take his shower first, he said cheerily; Lionel would be next, if he wanted. Lionel dressed while Tim sang in the shower. It was still snowing, but the snow had become wetter, almost sleet. The streets were slushy. Lionel and Tim Dwyer walked to the supermarket for breakfast. There was a counter there which served coffee and doughnuts, beside the checkouts. Tim, like everyone else at the counter, lit a cigarette. Lionel couldn't finish his doughnut. He kept looking around for a newspaper even though he had already ascertained that there were none for sale anywhere in the supermarket. He had not seen any boxes outside, either. When he had finished his coffee, he watched Tim go to the cash and carefully count out a dollar ninety-five cents for his own coffee and doughnut. Lionel fumbled for his wallet and followed him and paid for his own. He was thinking about his publisher, and what he would say to him when he called him that afternoon.

They walked across the parking lot and Lionel watched his shoes whitening with salt. He had not brought any boots, just these shiny brogues, now no longer shiny. He felt an icy tongue of water licking the sole of his foot.

They met the local member of the provincial parliament after some waiting outside her office, when she showed up for work. She shook Lionel's hand and said she was enormously pleased to have him in the community, and especially the arts community, which was very strong there, would be very pleased to get this recognition, and she had to get immediately to work.

Lionel lunched with Tim Dwyer in a diner. He asked Tim if there was anywhere where he could get a newspaper and Tim was proud to tell him that in Goolie's Smokers World, the smoke shop where Lionel was scheduled to do his signing that afternoon, there were newspapers from all over the province.

"What about the *Globe?*"

"The *Globe and Mail?* Sure. I would think she would have that."

"I'm kind of used to reading it every morning. Makes me feel a bit lost if I don't."

"Oh, I'm sure Goolie will have it. I'm pretty well one hundred per cent positive she'll have it." Tim paused, then said, "At least yesterday's, if not today's."

"Oh." Lionel chewed on a French fry and swallowed. "Tim. I've read yesterday's. I was in the metropolis of Wolfville yesterday. They had it there." He shook his shoulders to relax them and said as if to himself, "That's okay, though. It's no problem. I don't really need it or anything." He stared through the streaked window at the parking lot, the trucks leaving ruts in the slush. He could see a sign, at the end of the street, to the highway, the highway that would lead to Halifax, and the airport. There had been a basement bar in Halifax that he had rather liked. If he had to spend another night, he would rather do it in Halifax, a significant portion of it in that basement bar. The waiters there had been so unimaginably vast and red-haired he had had a brief vision of being enveloped in them, swallowed in their guts; such imaginings, he guessed, were rather like vertigo, the urge to throw oneself off a building.

He went back to rehearsing his voice-mail message to Jack Thalamus, enumerating his sufferings. And he wanted to talk to Sandra. It was as if he had missed too many nights of sleep and Sandra's voice would make the feeling go away. He wondered if it would be the wrong move to call her from a payphone. It was the middle of the day and she would be busy. And politically it would be wrong, right now. He said, "This smoke shop. I thought I was going to be signing in a bookstore."

"Oh it is a bookstore. It's like a magazine shop. Goolie has about a zillion magazines in there, anything you care to read. And cards and things. It's the closest thing we have to a bookstore, anyway." Tim was fingering his pack of cigarettes. "I'll wait till you're done." He laid them gently on the check tablecloth.

"But does he actually sell any books there?"

"Sure she does. Sure. I would think so, anyway. I'm sure I've seen a book in there. At special times, you know, when there's a book of local interest, or a special case like this."

"So he has copies of my book?"

"Forty of 'em. Are you done?"

"Forty? *Forty?* Why on earth did he take forty copies?"

"She. Goolie's a she. Is that a lot? We didn't know. Do you mind if I smoke now?"

"She'll never sell them. We're lucky if we sell forty copies at a bookstore signing in Toronto. And you know, this is kind of an experimental novel, Tim. It's difficult even for . . . How many people live in this town?"

"Oh, you'd be surprised how many people turn out to a thing like this." Tim's fingers closed over the cigarette pack; his other hand reached for a lighter.

"In a snowstorm? She'll have to return them all. But listen, Tim, this could be a problem for her. If I sign them, my publisher won't take them back. He considers them damaged if they're signed. She could lose quite a lot of money over this."

"Well, we'll just let Goolie decide what she wants to do about that." Tim lit his cigarette and took a deep drag. He exhaled with his eyes closed. "Haaaaah. Don't worry so much, Lionel. Everything will be fine. We'll just see what happens." Tim looked at his watch importantly. "Now. Here's a question for you. Did your publisher give you any expense money for meals and such? Would he by chance look very closely at your receipts to see if your lunch bill included mine?"

Before the signing was the live interview on the local community cable channel, which was in a two-storey concrete block owned by the provincial government. The TV station, according to the sign outside, was also run by Employment and Immigration, in particular by a project called "Fundy Works!" They had to walk there, too, but it wasn't far. They passed a ferry terminal, which made Lionel wonder about alternate means of escape after the reading, but Tim explained to him that the ferry went to the U.S.A., which would take him even farther away from Halifax. The sleet had turned to rain. Lionel's feet, both feet, were unequivocally wet now. The studio was cold. The sad little man who interviewed him had a moustache and a bright yellow cardigan, and shook his hand very solemnly. "I'm very much looking forward to reading your book," he said. "I work entirely as a volunteer here, because I'm interested, and I think it's important to the community. I'm a crafter."

"Ah," said Lionel.

"We have a very active community here."

"Uh-huh," said Lionel. "I'm not sure I follow you."

"Of crafters."

"Yes." They were being seated on two metal office chairs which formed the set. There was a full ashtray and two Coke cans on the coffee table. A teenager with long hair was clipping on Lionel's lapel mike. Lionel wondered if the teenager was going to remove the cans and the ashtray, or if the coffee table was not going to be in the shot. "I'm not sure I know what crafters are. I'm sorry."

"Oh, any kind of crafter. We have some stained-glass makers. Some weavers. And you've probably heard about the very active puppeteering community."

"Oh, *crafts*. I see. That's good. That's terrific."

The man with the moustache, whose name Lionel was now thinking was Bob, but it may have been Trevor or Kevin, one of the names he always confused, was shading his eyes against the lights and squinting at the control booth. He called out, "Are we set, Danny?"

Danny was not. They waited for something unexplained for five, then ten, then fifteen minutes. Lionel's feet were numb. He began to shiver. He could see Tim Dwyer in the control room, sitting on the edge of a chair and laughing with the technician. The technician had his hands folded behind his head and his feet on the control panel.

"I thought this was live?" said Lionel.

"Oh, it is, once we get going," said Bob or Trevor or Kevin. (*Justin*, thought Lionel suddenly, and decided on that.)

"But what about the other programming? Or are we just waiting for that?"

Justin looked at him. "What do you mean?"

"How do you slot it in?"

"I don't get you."

"Are there other programs?"

"Oh no. Not yet. We just broadcast when there's something important going on. This will be the first show of the day."

"Of the week," called out the teenager, who was lighting a cigarette.

"And then there's nothing until the city hall meeting later this evening, so we can start any time we want. Are we ready, Danny? Okay, looks like we're set. Is there anything you want me to ask you or you want to say in particular?"

"No."

"All right then. Could you tell me your name one more time?"

Lionel pronounced it very carefully several times, while Justin attempted to repeat it. He came close enough. Then he turned to the camera and said, "Welcome to 'Spotlight on Yarmouth.' I'm Kevin MacNamara, and with me today is Lionel Barsit— Bantimellow."

"Baratelli," said Lionel, thinking, *Kevin, remember that, it's Kevin.*

Kevin laughed and shook his head. "Well that is a tough one, you must admit. How about I just call you Lionel? Okay? Okay. Lionel. Lionel, we're very happy to have you here in the community, and you know we have a very active arts community here, so I was thinking the members of the community would like to hear where you personally get your inspiration."

Lionel was silent for a long moment. Finally he said, "Well, Kevin. I didn't expect the Spanish Inquisition." He gave a short laugh.

Kevin just smiled.

When Lionel and Tim emerged from the studio the temperature had dropped and it had begun to snow again. The snow was accumulating on the hardening runnels of slush. "This is all going to freeze right up," said Tim gleefully. "Looks like we're in for an ugly night." A pickup truck skidded all the way down the main street. There were no people on the sidewalk. "If the snow activity continues."

Snow, thought Lionel, *you cretin, not snow activity, just plain snow.* He said, "Where is the reading, this evening?"

"Public library. And I have wine and some sandwiches catered up, enough for the first fifty people or so, after that they're on their own. So it will be strictly on a first-come-first-served basis."

Lionel tried to resist responding to this, but there was snow melting in his collar, his feet were cold, and this time he could not. "Not *basis*, Tim," he said with sudden energy. "Just first come first served. You don't need to say basis."

Tim jerked his face towards Lionel's, a fixed smile on it, as if he thought Lionel might be joking. Tim laughed a little and Lionel did not and Tim's smile dropped.

Lionel felt instant guilt. He tried to smile and said, "I'm kind of obsessed with this kind of thing."

Tim nodded, smiling again, and Lionel could tell he was hurt. "Come to think of it, I guess you're right."

"Never mind me."

"No, no, I'll remember that, I really will. It never occurred to me before. Thank you, Lionel."

Lionel felt queasy with nastiness. He reminded himself that Tim had in fact been more than generous to him and had put him up in his own house and given him the large part of a bottle of Scotch which must have been a serious financial investment for someone who had been on the dole for so long. He would have to remember to give him a bottle as a gift before he left. Another gust of wind blew snow into his eyes. He turned his coat collar up. "Tim, if this storm picks up . . . Where do you think the audience will come from? Is it the teachers' college students you're counting on?"

"Teachers' college?"

"Isn't there a teachers' college?"

"There was. It closed last year. Didn't you hear? There was all kinds of ruckus about it."

"It closed? There's no teachers' college?"

"Well there *was*. Until the Tories came in and —"

"What about the Acadian university? Is that still going?"

"What's that? St. Anne's you mean?"

"I guess so. I heard there was a French-speaking college."

"Yup, that's the one. You think they might come?"

"That's what I'm asking you."

"Oh. Well, they keep pretty much to themselves. They're pretty far out of town, you know. And they're pretty big on all French, only French, you know what I mean?"

"I see."

"Also, it's pretty close to Christmas. I think their classes are all finished. And they all go home to their families in the country for Christmas, you know, they're all Catholics, and Christmas is a pretty big deal. But you never know." Tim was trying to light a cigarette amid gusts of wind. "A couple of them might show up."

"So who are you counting on, exactly? To show up?"

"Oh, the community. The arts community is very —"

"Very strong here, yes, Tim, you know, fifty people, that's an awfully high estimate. I mean, in my experience literary readings don't draw very many people in the best of weather, even in large cities. You might even think about cancelling this event."

"Cancelling?" Tim chuckled. "Oh, I wouldn't do that to you, Lionel." He clapped him on the shoulder, and they stepped into the street. Ice cracked under Lionel's shoes.

Goolie's was in a strip mall across from the railway station. As they crossed the parking lot, Lionel glanced at the railway station and realized that there could possibly be a train back to Halifax that very evening, one that he could possibly get on immediately after the reading, and not have to stay another night on Tim Dwyer's couch while waiting for the next day's bus. He asked Tim about this, who laughed and said, "*Trains?* Oh, my dear man, there haven't been trains here for years and years and years and years." They both stopped and stared at the railway station for a silent moment, and Lionel saw that it was indeed cracked and window-less. Tim shouted above the wind, "They keep talking about making it into a museum. But nothing ever seems to happen. That was before the Tories got in."

They turned back to the small shop with two large racks of magazines, empty of people. The wind was blowing so hard it was difficult to open the glass door. Lionel and Tim stepped in and stamped the snow off their feet; Lionel's glasses fogged up immediately, so he removed them and took in the scene in soft focus. There was a card table set up with about twenty copies of Lionel's book, *Vague City*, on it. Scotch-taped to the table was a photocopy of the publicity photograph Jack Thalamus had sent ahead of him. There was a cardboard box with the Loon Lake colophon all over it next to the table; Lionel felt the queasiness again as he contemplated how many pristine books he would be asked to desecrate.

"Well I am *so* glad to meet you." A short woman with a tower of grey hair and large plastic glasses was stubbing out a cigarette in an ashtray on the counter. She waddled out and pressed Lionel's hand in both of hers. "It's an honour. A real honour."

"Thank you," said Lionel, startled.

"How you doing, Goolie?" said Tim Dwyer.

"Oh, surviving, Tim. Surviving." She coughed a wheezy smoker's cough. "I've got a table all set up for you." She put a hand in the small of Lionel's back and guided him towards the card table. She inserted him in the small space between it and a magazine rack. "Let me take your coat."

"Really," said Lionel, sitting with difficulty behind the table, "I'm not sure I'll have to sit for long. If no one comes in I suggest we scrap the whole thing."

"Oh," chorused Tim and Goolie, "you never know."

Goolie lit a cigarette. "We're so pleased to have you here. I haven't looked at your book yet, but I'm looking forward to reading it. I'm a big reader, you know? I guess I'm just addicted to it."

Lionel looked up at the two people standing over him. Sitting, he felt like a small child, especially dressed up in his jacket and tie, which was probably the only jacket and tie being worn in the whole of Yarmouth. He said to Goolie, "So how did you get interested in this? I mean, how did you hear about this book?"

"Oh Tim told me. Tim told me he'd set this whole thing up and you needed a place to do a signing, so I was happy to buy some copies."

Lionel looked out at the darkening window, the snow blown against it. "Ah. About those copies. There's a problem you may not be aware of if I sign them all. I mean, you've taken on a lot of copies, and we may not sell that many on a day like today. In fact . . ." He turned his head to face into a copy of *Recreational Vehicles* on the rack. "We may not sell any, on a day like today. I mean . . ." He tried to chuckle. "I wouldn't blame people here if they weren't all that interested in me, you know, not having heard much about me or . . . anyway, the problem is, if I sign all these books you won't be able to return them to my publisher. He considers them spoiled."

Goolie smiled widely, "Oh, that's all right dear. I don't do it to make any money. I like to contribute in any way I can to the community."

Tim said, "Goolie is a *great* supporter of the community."

"I see." Lionel nodded. "Kind of like a charity."

"Well," said Goolie, "I figure we all have a responsibility to give back in some way. To the —"

"Community," said Lionel. "Got you."

"I'll get you a pen."

"Well, why don't we just wait and see if anyone comes in first. What do you think?"

"Well, you're all set then?" said Tim. "I'll see you in two hours." He zipped up his parka.

"Two *hours?*" Lionel laughed giddily. "Tim, there's really no point in my waiting here —"

"Well, that's what I advertised in the flyers. It would be rude to have someone come in at a quarter to five and have you gone, now, wouldn't it? I've got some errands to run, anyway." He waved cheerily at Goolie. "You take good care of my man, now, love."

Goolie began to cough violently. Between coughs, she sputtered, "You be a good boy now, Tim." After he had gone out into the storm, she coughed with heaving shudders until the sound was not as wet and phlegmy, and she was just hacking, a sound like paper tearing. Finally, gasping and wiping her mouth, she said, "He's such a sweet boy, really."

"Yes, he certainly is."

Lionel and Goolie smiled at each other for a long moment, Goolie warmly, Lionel tightly. He looked at his watch. Three minutes of his two-hour book signing had passed. He pushed the table out and rose. "Do you have the *Globe and Mail?*"

"No, dear."

"Ah." He took in a rack of magazine titles. They included *Canadian Sewing, Knitter's Digest* and *Needle Art.* He was moving to the next row, which included more promising pictures of guns and motorcycles, when Goolie said, "Don't you think you'd better stay behind the table? Otherwise people might think you'd gone, or they wouldn't know who you were, you know?"

Instinctively, Lionel moved back to his seat, then remembered that he was a grown-up and didn't actually have to do everything the people in Yarmouth told him to do. "I promise you I will sit down if someone comes in."

And someone did come in, at that moment, a huge young man in an army parka. He had a beard and long hair and a military beret. He looked away from Lionel's jacket and tie in embarrassment or fear, and muttered, "Mom."

Lionel was introduced and shook hands with Goolie's son, whose face grew dark red at the contact and stared at the carpeted floor.

"Pretty bad storm out there." said Lionel.

"Uh." The boy nodded vigorously, his eyes darting up to his mother and back down to the floor. Then he started trying to say something. "I, uh, I, s-s-s —" He clutched at the counter and stopped.

"It's all right, Ashley," said his mother gently. "Just take it easy."

"I s-s-s." He shook his head, grinned at Lionel quickly and started again. "I s-s-s, huh, s-s —"

"Lots of time, Ash," said Goolie.

"Yup, huh, s-saw you."

Lionel, smiling as much as he could, said, "Me? You saw me?"

"Yup. On tee, teevee."

"Oh." Lionel nodded and smiled and kept on nodding. "Yes. Could have been me. I've been on a couple of shows. Which one was it?"

"Oh." The bear-like young man had not taken his parka or his hat off, and snow was melting and running down in streaks of water. Drops of water hung in his beard. "Don't know. It was like a p-p-p, bunch of people sitting around. I thought you were p-p-pretty cool. You were all right." He giggled and swallowed. His face was still glowing like embers.

"A panel. Yes. That's the kind of thing I — was it "Pamela Wallin," maybe? I did that recently." Suddenly Lionel was eager to talk to someone about something he knew about and that someone else knew about. "Do you remember? Or it could have been "Imprint. "A rerun, maybe."

Ashley was shaking his head. "Yeah. I guess."

"Do you remember who the host was? A guy or a woman?"

Ashley shook his head. "It was like, l-l-late at night." He chortled or swallowed again, Lionel couldn't tell which. "I was" — he laughed and snorted — "I was half trashed."

Lionel smiled and shrugged and nodded and said, "Yes," as if to say, Well, of course, trashed, who isn't?

"I was right . . ." Ashley shook his head and drummed with his fingers on the counter, yelping a little as he laughed. "I was *right* ripped."

Lionel laughed and nodded again. This conversation subsided. Ashley went into the back room to do some assigned task for his mother. Lionel heard a radio being switched on, and for the next forty-five minutes they listened to the pop songs and the singing advertisements for used-car dealerships, and the announcements for meetings of the Four-H and the AA. Lionel perused several body-building magazines and *Outlaw Biker*. Goolie picked up a paperback Harlequin behind the counter and lit another cigarette.

No one entered the shop. Lionel sat back down at his table and looked out at the furious snow, then at his watch. He had decided that one hour of this would be more than generous to everybody, and he could tell Thalamus that he had at least made an effort, so he would wait another fifteen minutes and take off on his own and find a bar — he knew there would at least be a bar, somewhere — and compose a letter to Sandra. (In which he would be undoubtedly nostalgic but not entirely repentant, not without defending himself.) He might even not tell Goolie which bar he was heading for, so as to pass a couple of hours without the company of Tim Dwyer. He would be able to find the library on his own. He cleared his throat and said, "Listen, Mrs. Goolie —"

"Just Goolie, dear. It's what people call me."

"I'm about ready to —"

But the door opened with a squall of snow and a hunter in a moustache came in. Lionel knew he was a hunter because he wore camouflage pants and a camouflage jacket and a camouflage hat, and high rubber boots. Lionel scuttled behind his table, sat down and smiled at him. The man looked at him uncertainly, smiled quickly and looked away.

"How you doin', Stewart?" said Goolie.

"Not too bad, Goolie."

"*Guns and Ammo?*"

"If it's in."

"New one's just in. Over there."

The man had to walk past Lionel, who felt unbelievably ridiculous in his jacket and tie and his pile of books. The man tried not to look at him. Nobody made any attempt to explain Lionel's presence. As quickly as he could, and starting to blush as well, as if there was someone in the room with a hideous disfigurement that should not be noticed, the hunter paid for his copy of *Guns and Ammo* and pushed off into the storm.

"See?" said Goolie. "People still drop in, even in a storm."

Lionel stood up. "Is there a payphone I could use? For a long-distance call?"

She looked puzzled. "Long-distance? Right now?"

"Yes. Sorry. There's just a little business thing I was supposed to check on today. In Toronto."

"Oh. Well, there is, just outside, but . . . How are you going to call long-distance from the payphone? You want some change, dear?" She opened the cash register drawer. "I'll see what I have."

"No no. I have a calling card. Thanks anyway." He took his coat from the hook and stepped into the street. Immediately, there was snow in his eyes; it was coming horizontally across the parking lot, having gathered speed coming across the railway tracks and the field before that. His eyes narrowed, his coat flapping as he tried to do up the buttons, Lionel half ran to the payphone. It was under the overhang of the strip mall, and its two plastic sides provided a little protection. Lionel was still in view of the smoke shop, so he tried to smile as he fumbled with his calling card and it refused to swipe and he had to punch in a string of about seventy-five digits which he kept screwing up and beginning again because his fingers were so cold. Finally, the phone in the offices of Loon Lake publishing began to ring, and was answered by Elizabeth, who was Jack Thalamus's publicist and copy editor and cover designer and secretary, and also wife. She was very pleased to hear from Lionel, and suitably dismayed to hear that things were not exactly as Lionel had desired them. She didn't go quite so far as apologizing for his lodgings, which she must have arranged herself, but she was at least mothering about it. "Oh well," she said brightly, "if you can just stick it out for this last night, only one more night and then it's back to Halifax tomorrow and the plane home the next day, right? *That* isn't so bad, is it?"

Jack, unfortunately, was out, and probably would be out all afternoon.

Lionel instructed Elizabeth to inform Jack that there was no teachers' college in Yarmouth and had not been for several years, and that the Acadian university was closed for the Christmas holidays. "Make sure he knows that, would you, please, Liz? And tell him that I'll be calling back later."

"Certainly, Lionel. Of course I will. About what, in particular?"

"To discuss that with him."

Elizabeth paused. "To discuss what?"

"To discuss the fact that there is no university or college in this town where I am booked to do my reading."

"Yes. Well, I'll be sure to tell him that myself."

"And so will I. Tell him I would be happy to discuss this at some length. And I will. And I will call back later this afternoon, or this evening if necessary, to discuss this with him. All right?"

Lionel hung up. He had begun to shiver and was going to go back inside but the sight of the dark old railway station, once a pretty building, with its brick and its carved wooden gables, with its cracked panes and the snow building against it, made him feel like crying. He took a deep breath and punched his codes in again and dialled Sandra's number, the number of the apartment where he was no longer staying.

She was home. She said, "Hellooo!" so cheerily it made Lionel start.

"Hello?"

"Helloo-oo," she said impatiently.

"Hi. It's me."

"Hi. Where are you? Are you in a crowded place?"

"No. No I could by no stretch of the imagination be said to be in a crowded place. I'm in a parking lot in a blizzard in Yarmouth."

"Where's that? Is this part of your tour?"

"In Nova Scotia. Yes. It's awful. I'm miserable."

"Oh. No. Listen, I can't really talk right now."

"I know." Lionel bit his lip and looked around the parking lot. The last parked pickup was pulling out. He looked along the railway tracks and squinted, as if he could see Halifax at the end of them. He felt close to tears. "I know, sweetheart. Just talk to me for a few minutes. I haven't talked to anyone for two days, and I'm fucking miserable. I'm really miserable. This whole thing is a waste of time. There are no people. They've even closed down the teachers' college. Everyone I meet is slightly retarded, I think, I think it must be the whole town, they keep repeating the word 'community,' it's some kind of fucking *mantra*. I'm sitting alone in this smoke shop to do a signing and when people come in they're embarrassed that I look so sad, which makes me embarrassed and then I look sadder and then they're more embarrassed. I wish I was home."

"Oh. I'm sorry. That's awful."

"Yes," said Lionel. "And I'm sorry to bother you in the middle of the day. I just had to tell someone about it. I thought you'd laugh."

There was a long silence.

Lionel said, "I know I'm not supposed to be calling you at all. I know. I'm sorry. But I think of you."

At the other end of the expensive midday connection, Sandra sighed. "Well. I think of you, too. But I'm trying not to."

"I know. I know. I'm sorry."

"I mean."

"Yes?"

Another sigh.

He said, "You mean what?"

"It's just that . . . well, you're the one who wanted us to be apart in the first place."

"Sweetheart, it's not that I want us to be apart for good, you know that, Christ, how many times do we have to go through this, it's just a brief period, a space, you know, besides, I'm —"

"And you know that I told you I don't believe in that, I don't do trial separations, I think they're — anyway, I don't need this now, I don't want to be arguing with you on the phone about this, again."

"I assure you, neither do I, I promise you I don't. I just called because I wanted to hear your voice, and —"

"Lionel, don't do this to me. I've been doing so well. I'm just starting to — I've been out and about and I'm, I'm having a good time."

"Good. That's good. I'm glad to hear it."

"Well. Now you call me up and try to make me . . . I don't know. I think it's kind of mean."

"What? Trying to make you what? I'm not trying to make you anything. I'm not trying to make you feel bad. I'm not that manipulative, honestly, I'm not. I just felt lonely and wanted to talk to you."

"Okay." She was silent for a moment. "I'll have to think about that."

"Okay." Lionel smiled and waved into the shop at Goolie, who was looking anxiously at him. He stamped his feet and wiggled his fingers in his pockets. The phone was wedged at his shoulder. "Look. I'm sorry. I'm sorry for everything."

A long pause, and then she said, "How about I just think about this for a while. And I call you back later."

"You can't call me back. I'm in a payphone in a parking lot, and I don't know where I'll be later. I'll call you back."

"Okay."

"Okay, when?"

"In, I don't know, whenever you like. Just let me get my head around this."

"Okay. Okay. I'll talk to you later. Bye."

Lionel hung up and smiled through the window at Goolie. No one had come or gone from the store. He couldn't face going back in. He held up his finger to say "One more phone call," and Goolie smiled and nodded. His fingers shook so much with cold he had to punch in his code number three times. He dialled his own number, the voice-mail box he was renting while he stayed with Brotman, got his message, punched in his voice-mail code. He expected a chain of messages; he was remembering Toronto, already, as an endless connection of cocktail parties and gossipy business lunches and earnest discussions of new media technology and the Gnostic gospels, which of course it wasn't, as was proved by the fact that there was only one message. It was from his agent, Michiyo, and sounded rather frantic. "What are we going to do about this Pyramid deal?" she said. "Aren't you checking your messages? *Please* call me right away, wherever you are."

Lionel's heart began to beat faster. His teeth were chattering as well, but that could have been the cold. The Pyramid deal had been done for months. For *months*. Everyone *knew*, by now, that Pyramid Pictures had the option and were poised at any moment to buy the rights, the outright rights; the trade media had reported on this; the goddam *Globe* had reported on this. There was the goddam *car* he had gone and bought.

Of course Michiyo didn't leave her number, so he had to use his calling card once again to use directory assistance in Toronto, and then to call her.

She answered right away. "Well," she said, as if angry at him, "what are we going to do?"

"About what? I have no idea what you're talking about. Is something wrong with the Pyramid deal?"

"Well, I would assume so. Haven't you read the paper?"

"The paper — no, no I haven't, I —"

"Lionel, honestly, you really *should* read the paper, you know, you can really take this ivory tower shit too far."

"Michiyo," Lionel almost shouted, "believe me, there is *nothing* deliberate in this, I am in fucking Yarmouth Nova Scotia, in a fucking parking lot in a blizzard, and I cannot get a fucking paper because I am on this tour in the middle of nowhere which Loon Lake has booked for me, which is the publisher that *you* encouraged me to go with, so don't — Jesus, listen, let's stop this, what *is* it, anyway?"

"All right. Okay. Calm down. The story is that Pyramid has just gone down. It was in this morning's paper."

"What do you mean, gone down?"

"Tits up. Game over. And they haven't paid you yet. Have they even paid you for the option?"

Lionel closed his eyes and felt the snow beating against his eyelids. It was turning into hard little pellets, perhaps hail or freezing rain. He said, "Jesus fucking Christ almighty."

"Well, actually, it's not quite true that they've declared bankruptcy, they haven't, yet, they've just applied for protection, and they're talking about restructuring, which sounds bad to me. So it could work out. There are all kinds of rescuers people are talking about, they're talking to Cineplex Odeon about a partnership deal, who knows, something could happen. But in the meantime you're going to wait for your money, unless we do something else."

"Like what?"

"Well, I'm taking a meeting this afternoon with Franco Goseiwicz. I could pitch it to him. I could just offer it to him, for less than Pyramid offered, of course, and say it was like a fire sale. Bankruptcy sale. I know he likes you and he loves to score anything he could off Pyramid and it could just work."

"Shit." Lionel thought about this for a second. "But we've signed a contract with Pyramid. For the option. We'd be . . . you can't do that until you know."

"Well, yes. We'd be just assuming that Pyramid goes under. If it does, then no one's going to bother us about it, they won't be able to pay for our deal anyway. The only thing to worry about would be if the restructuring works."

Lionel was silent. The door of Goolie's Smokers' World opened and Goolie put her tower of grey hair into the air. "Are you okay, Lionel?" she called.

"Yes, fine thanks. Sorry about this, I'll be right in. Just some business that's just come up."

"You must be freezing, dear."

"Who is that?" said Michiyo.

"I've got to go. I'm supposed to be doing a book signing. Look, I don't know. Do whatever you think is best. If you want to sell it again, do it, and get whatever you can for it. Don't go under . . . I don't know, say eight. Eighty-five hundred."

"I'll try. I'll see what I can do."

Lionel sighed. "And I'll lose the car."

"I'm sorry about this, Lionel. These things happen."

"Yeah. That's life, I guess. Just ask around first to see if you really think they're going under for sure."

"Of course. I'll let you know. By the way, I also had a message from *Edge*, they were trying to get hold of you."

"Oh, wonderful. Terrific. Did they say what about? They have a story of mine. The Christmas story. It's about to come out."

"Yeah, it was something about that. It's not coming out."

"It's not," said Lionel. "It's not coming out." Rather than bellowing in primal anguish, he was silent. It was too absurd. He opened his mouth wide and turned it up to the falling snow. He wondered what phrase or expression he could use to Michiyo to best convey his inability to even muster the requisite horror and outrage at this news, what would best conjure a kind of pathos, the kind of devastated battlefield beauty of his inner spaces at this news, how to convey to her the grimness of his realization that he was strangely not surprised at this news, not surprised, at this point, that the one sure piece of income that he could count on for Christmas, the one assignment he had miraculously completed and which had been astonishingly accepted without major revisions, was now also in jeopardy. Weakly, he said, "Did they mention why it's not coming out?"

"You'll have to ask them. I didn't handle that for you, if you recall." Michiyo hesitated, then relented. "They said something about the lawyers. It was too dangerous."

"Did they say whether they were going to pay me in full, or am I going to have to sue them?"

"I have no idea. You'll have to —"

"I know. I know. All right. I can't think about that right now. I can't face it. One thing at a time. You go ahead and sell my soul to Goseiwicz."

"I'll see what I can do."

"Thanks, Michiyo." Lionel hung up and staggered against the wind back into the shop, where his glasses fogged up again.

"Everything all right?" said Goolie.

Lionel puffed out his cheeks. "Not really. A bit of a crisis in Toronto."

"I'm sorry to hear that. Would you like another cup of coffee?"

"No, thank you." Lionel sat back down at his card table and put his head in his hands. There were fifty minutes left in his book signing, and then Tim Dwyer would be back to take him out for another pizza slice or souvlaki, which Lionel would pay for, and then there would be the gala festivities of the reading at the public library, possibly followed by a night of wild debauchery at Passages or the Wagon Wheel Lounge or on Tim Dwyer's linoleum. He tried to think about this so as not to think about Sandra or Michiyo or the cowards at *Edge* or that shark Goseiwicz whom he had vowed he would never be associated with or losing the car or the prospect of being sued by Pyramid Productions. His head, he realized, was like a computer game bristling with hidden lasers and fanged things; it was just a question of navigating the right path through the bad thoughts without getting zapped.

119

The bell on the door rang and another man with a moustache and a parka came in. He made straight for Lionel's table. "Who's the fellow from Tronno? How the hell are you?" He pumped Lionel's hand, and then whipped out of the parka a copy of *Vague City*. "I was so excited about this fellow from Tronno coming down I was in here yesterday to get a copy of the book before they all sold out. Wasn't I, Goolie?" He slammed it on the table before Lionel, with a ballpoint pen in the other hand. "There you go. Do the honours."

"Thank you," said Lionel, taking his own fountain pen from his breast pocket. "Thank you very much. I'm flattered." He felt himself blushing: the first genuine pleasure he had had on this trip. "Who shall I sign it to?"

"Dave. Dave Pottie. Pleased to meet you."

"And you." Lionel wrote, *for Dave, with much gratitude.* "Are you from around here, Dave?"

"Born and bred. Just like Goolie here. Eh Goolie? Now let me tell you a story you would find inner-esting. On your way into town you would have passed a row of beautiful old wooden hous-es, just off the one-o-three, off Hardscratch Road? Or you would have come on the one-o-one, coming from Digby, anyway, if you had of come off the one-o-three you would have seen two big old wooden houses, one blue, one green — you know the ones? Did you see the green one? Anyway, that green one, that used to belong to a guy called Andrew Pottie, no relation. Now. Andrew Pottie." Dave Pottie paused, one finger raised as if to presage the revealing of the unbelievable truth about Andrew Pottie. Lionel felt his own smile waning, and revived it with a facial tightening. "Andrew Pottie, now it's not true to say he's no relation to me, because in fact he was my uncle's cousin, which would make him my what?"

He turned to Goolie, who looked at the ceiling and thought.

"Make him your . . . second cousin?"

"Is that right?"

"I'm not sure," said Lionel, whose smile was now a rictus. He decided to let it drop.

"Anyway, Andrew Pottie had a successful car dealership here, and one day, god knows why, just decides to chuck the whole thing. And *he* winup to Tronno, — this would have been five, six years ago now — got himself into the *printing* business there, and last we heard, incredible, doing just great, owns his own company and everything." Dave Pottie beamed. "Now I don't hear from him much myself, but Dave Stewart, works in the federal building, says he just heard that he'd bought a house, brand new house, and everything. So I guess he likes it up there."

Lionel nodded sagely. He had an impulse to say "hup," in an intake of breath, which he suspected was the appropriate response, but would have felt like a fraud. He decided to try this after a few drinks. He said, "Is that right?" Which did seem to please Dave Pottie, who smiled even harder.

"Now," said Dave Pottie, leaning over Lionel's table, "I'll tell you about another guy from around here. He was *from* Tronno, or at least his family was, and they come down here about seventy-six seventy-seven, somewhere around there. Anyway."

This took Lionel pretty well to the end of his signing period. Dave Pottie suddenly decided he had to go, after about half an hour. He interrupted his own story to rush out into the snow. It was now dark. "Well," said Lionel, rising and stretching. "I guess Tim will be back to pick me up any minute now."

"That's what he said," said Goolie. "Around five."

"Well, I have to make one more phone call. So I'll be in the parking lot."

Again Lionel felt close to tears as he half ran to the phone booth, trying to button his coat as he ran. The drifts around the abandoned train station had risen to the window ledges. He found his calling card and dialled Sandra. He was surprised by how relieved he felt when she answered. "Hi," he said, "me again."

She exhaled, which could have been a sigh, and said, "Hi Lionel."

"Are you mad at me? Please don't be mad at me."

"No. I'm not mad. I was just a little confused, that's all." Her voice did sound gentler. "How was your signing?"

Very rapidly, and in growing excitement, Lionel told her the story of the signing, and repeated Dave Pottie's stories, beginning to giggle, which made her giggle too. When he had calmed down he was relaxed enough to tell her about his abandonment by *Edge* and the Pyramid crisis. But she didn't respond to this quite the way he wanted. She said, "I don't know how I'm supposed to help you with that. I don't know what you want me to say."

"Nothing," said Lionel. "I don't want you to say anything. I don't know what to do, that's all."

"Well I don't know what you should do."

"No. No I didn't expect you would. I wasn't calling for advice. Just . . ."

"Just support, I guess."

"Yes. It's just bad news, that's all. I wanted to tell someone about it."

Sandra didn't reply.

"Are you mad at me," said Lionel, "because I'm coming to you for support and I was the one who . . ."

"Who what?"

"Who, you know, has been causing all the problems lately, and stuff. All the bad stuff."

She was silent a long time. Then she said, "I want to give you support. Believe me I do. I'm just trying to keep my distance a little. I thought that's what you wanted."

"Yes," said Lionel. He heard a siren and registered being impressed that there was a fire station or a police station or whatever it was with a siren. It comforted him a little. "It was what I wanted. And I completely understand what you're saying. I know. I'm sorry to be so confusing." He saw Tim Dwyer approaching across the parking lot, slipping on the ice under the snow. "Anyway. I'd better go."

"Okay."

"Maybe I'll call you later?"

"Okay."

"Is that okay?"

"Sure. I guess. That's fine."

"Okay. Thanks for talking. I'd better go."

"Lionel?"

"Yes."

"It's good to talk to you."

Lionel smiled in the wind. "Me, too. Thanks."

He had some wings and fries in Lanny's Roadhouse and Live Music Fridays with Tim Dwyer. Lionel had two pints of beer and felt sleepy. Then they tried to walk the two blocks to the library.

The slush that had been on the streets earlier in the day had frozen, and the snow had fallen on top of it, so they both slipped and fell twice. The library building was dark. "Now," said Tim, as they approached, "Eleanor said she'd meet us here, and she has the sandwiches."

They waited at a back door, in the parking lot, for Eleanor the librarian to arrive. There was a cone of yellow light from a streetlamp for them to stand in. They watched a heavy branch fall from a tree and split into two logs on the parking lot, blocking two parking spaces.

"Kind of a good thing," said Lionel, "that no one's here, or we would have seen a car get wrecked."

"Now this is true," said Tim. "There's a good side to everything, I guess. *Hup.* Got to see the silver lining, Lionel."

The reading was to start at eight; Eleanor showed up at five to eight. Lionel and Tim helped her unload vast trays of catered sandwiches and two large bottles of wine that had been made by Nova Scotia vineyards. Tim was unable to inform Lionel of the exact location of any Nova Scotia vineyards, but he assured him that there were many. They followed Eleanor through the dark corridors of the library, which smelled of schoolchildren. Eleanor switched on lights as she went, illuminating bright crayon drawings tacked to the walls.

She switched on the lights in a large carpeted room with stacks of chairs against one wall. Tim energetically began to arrange rows of chairs. He had set up three rows of ten chairs before Lionel gently stopped him.

At 8:15, Tim said, "We'll just give it some time. People may be having a hard time getting here on time, with the storm."

Eleanor the librarian was very pleasant, and mentioned to Lionel that she had recently read a book by Margaret Atwood, which impressed him enough that he made no bilious comment about Atwood's writing or personality, which he would have been expected to do in Toronto, and probably would have, even though he rather admired Margaret Atwood. He was trying to drink the Nova Scotian wine, which tasted like the fluoride mixture the dentist used to put on his teeth when he was a child. He put the glass aside.

At 8:30, they heard a clatter of boots on the outside stairs and the door opened and Kevin came in, the little moustachioed crafter from the television station. He had brought a pale wife named Kathleen. Everyone greeted them heartily, including Lionel. Lionel told them repeatedly how pleased he was that they had come, and he meant it. Kevin went immediately to the sandwich trays and began consuming with concentration, which pleased Tim and Lionel, who exhorted him and Eleanor and Kathleen to have more.

At 8:45, somewhat diminishing the feeling of conviviality that Tim and Kevin were enjoying over the sandwiches, Eleanor permitted Lionel to start. He read, as quickly as he could, what he thought was the safest passage in the text, which was a conversation between a philanderer and his wife and had an evolution vaguely reminiscent of a story, the closest he could come to a story, anyway. The passage had further in its favour that it contained no art jargon or robotic polysexual sex on dumpsters or in office cubicles, which was the kind of thing that recurred in most other scenes. There was, unfortunately, a subtle reference to an unemotional threesome the couple had had with a teenage girl, which Lionel hoped would pass unnoticed.

When he had finished his four listeners clapped politely, and Lionel paused for a moment, listening to the wind outside and the rattling windowpanes. The passage had read quicker than he had planned, and nobody made a move to leave. So he closed his folder and told a ghost story that he remembered from childhood. This did not cause as much of a splash as he had hoped. It ended with the same polite applause. And Lionel stood and said, "Thank you very much."

"Well," said Kevin, standing and stretching. "Thank you very much, Lionel. Most enjoyable. Can I give anyone a ride anywhere?"

Lionel looked at Tim.

"Sure," said Tim, "we're going back to my place."

"You're staying another night?" said Kevin.

"There's no bus till tomorrow," said Lionel.

"If that," said Kevin cheerily, and everybody laughed.

"What do you mean?"

"Well, sometimes they won't run the bus if the weather's bad enough. And it looks pretty bad."

"It's forecast to go on all night," said his wife, Kathleen. "They've already cancelled schools tomorrow."

"They're saying it might be a record," said Tim. "Thirty centimetres by morning, maybe more."

"You mean there might not be a bus tomorrow?" said Lionel, a little too loudly.

"That's right Lionel," said Tim, clapping him on the back. "You might just be trapped with us."

"But that's . . . that would be very bad for me. That would be *really* bad. I can't, I can't stay another day. I have to be back."

"Well," said Kevin, "suppose you might find someone driving in."

"Yes? Who?"

Everyone shrugged. "Well, Tim," said Eleanor, "what are we going to do with these sandwiches?"

"You want them?" said Tim to Kevin.

"Is there anyone," said Lionel, "I could call to find out about the bus?"

"You sure you don't want them?" said Kevin.

"What use would I have for fifty sandwiches?"

"Or is there a noticeboard," said Lionel, "where I could put up a note about looking for a ride?"

"I'd just wait till tomorrow, if I were you," said Eleanor. "You're not going to know anything tonight. Just see what happens."

"You got him just on your couch?" said Kevin.

"*Hup*," said Tim.

"We have a spare room, if he'd prefer a real bed tonight."

"Oh, I think we're fine, thanks anyway," said Tim.

"You have a spare bed?" said Lionel. "In a house?"

"You're more than welcome," said Kathleen.

"Probably be easier if he just stays with me," said Tim, "since all his stuff is there."

"Just one bag," said Lionel. "We could just pick it up on the way. I wouldn't want to inconvenience you for longer than one night, Tim. Might as well spread around the obligations a bit, ey?" He couldn't believe he'd just said "ey" like that. There it was, just slipped out. He hadn't even been trying.

"Would you rather that, Lionel?" said Tim, looking sad.

"Why not? Then I won't be in your way in the living room."

"Oh, you're not in my way. But if that's what you'd really like."

"We'll just go by Tim's place, then," said Lionel, hopping to the coat rack, "and pick up my stuff, if that's okay?"

Kevin and Kathleen lived in a large wood-frame house on a street of gabled houses, muffled by snow. The shingles were green, the trim yellow. "What's the date?" Lionel asked immediately.

"The date?"

"Of the house."

Kevin shrugged. "Pretty old, I would say."

"I would say very old. Beautiful house. I would say eighteen eighties, maybe even seventies. Beautiful."

They showed him his room, under sloping ceilings, with its mansard window. There was a calico quilt on the bed. "Perfect," said Lionel. "Thank you so much. This is really very kind of you." He yawned. "Very long day."

"Would you like anything?" said Kevin. "A little hot chocolate or something?"

"Well," said Lionel, hesitating. He knew exactly what he wanted. "You know what I *would* like, if you happen to have any, is, believe it or not, a drink. Of something alcoholic. You know, after a reading . . . If you have any wine or beer or anything like that."

Kevin frowned. "Oh. I'm not sure, to tell you the truth. We might have something in the liquor cabinet, sometimes people give us gifts and stuff, Christmas time . . ." He waddled back down the stairs. Lionel loosened his tie and followed him.

Kathleen was sitting in the living room with an old woman with white hair. There were hooked rugs on the wood floor and stained-glass panels and macramé plant holders hanging in the windows, and a naive painting of a wharf and a dory, in bright colours. Lionel found it striking. "Hello," he said.

"Hello," said the old woman, and smiled.

"This is Kevin's mom, Alice."

er for a couple of days, if he was snowed in here, and that he would not be able to work things out, and then he realized that he was already assuming that he wanted to work things out, that in fact this was why he was longing to get back to the city, to do this, and he didn't know what to feel about that. He took another sip of whisky and decided he felt good about it. He remembered her saying that it was good to talk to him this afternoon and this made him smile; it reduced the big black-shrouded piece of furniture that was Pyramid Productions from a grand piano to something like an armchair. You could at least step around it. He heard her say it again, *It's good to talk to you*, and he smiled, feeling sad and full of something expensive. He opened his eyes and looked at his watch: too late to call.

Kevin yawned. "Well," he said, yawning, "azhaa rhaahaa nougz, tomorrow."

"Sorry?" said Lionel.

"I say I'd better be thinking about turning in. Up early tomorrow." Kevin stood and stretched. "So we'll probably be out at work by the time you get up. So you can fix yourself breakfast and all?"

"Of course. You're sure that's . . ."

"No problem. We'll probably see you tomorrow evening, too." Kevin chuckled. "Since, aynaa zhenawaaa." He finished yawning and said, "Since I don't see any snowploughs about."

The bay windows of the living room were divided into panes by old wood, and the snow had gathered in triangles in the corner of each pane. It looked like the Christmas windows of touristy shops in Toronto, frosted with something in a spray can. The tree outside was distorted by the rippling glass, which made Lionel note, sleepily, that it must be the original glass. The tree's branches were

"How do you do?"

"Have a seat, Lionel."

"Let's see now," said Kevin, who was kneeling on tl head in a cupboard. "There's a little Bailey's, but tha kind of old. What's this, now? You drink Kahlua?"

"That's okay, Kevin," said Lionel. "Don't worry at not important."

"Here's a little *whisky*, but you probably wouldn't —

"Whisky?" said Lionel, leaning forward. "I would lc of that, if there's enough of it."

"Oh, sure." Kevin hauled himself to his feet, holdin tle of rye. "Are you sure that's what you'd like?"

Kevin's mother smiled placidly at Lionel as he took hi rye.

"I'll just leave the bottle with you," said Kevin.

"All righty," said Lionel. "Everyone's sure you don't join me?"

Kathleen giggled and put a hand to her mouth. "No, thar

The whisky tasted bright, sparkly, like the lights behir eyelids when you close them. He felt it burning his mou throat and then, with diminishing fierceness, his belly, an spreading through his arms and legs like a massage. He br deeply. He felt the reading receding a little. And then t pierced, before he could take defensive action, by the mem Michiyo and his collapsing film deal, and he closed his eye took more whisky and focused on pushing it away, hidi behind some big black fold, as you would an unwanted pie furniture. He tried to think of blackness, and succeeded for a ond, until he thought of Sandra, realizing that he would no heavily loaded with snow. And the snow was still coming, silently ramming the glass and dying in waves, dumb and insistent. The only sound was the roar of the furnace under their feet. No street noise came from outside, not even spinning tires. The whole town seemed muffled.

He slept as soon as he slid between the musty sheets under the quilt, in the dead silence of the attic room with the snow weighing on the roof.

He woke to a grey light. He looked out the window and saw more snow than he had ever seen in a city street, or indeed anywhere. It was like an immobile flood. There was snow covering the front steps of the houses. The cars had become white humps. It was still snowing.

Lionel rose and shivered and dressed. He ran his hand over his goatee, which needed a trim. It was becoming a beard. He went down the creaky stairs to the empty hall. He went into the empty kitchen and opened the fridge. He found coffee and a coffeemaker. He said hello to the old lady, Kevin's mother, who was sitting in the living room, knitting. He found a phone book and called the bus station, and got the recorded message saying that all buses had been cancelled. He stood at the kitchen window, looking at the whiteness, and thought of Pyramid Pictures and Tim Dwyer and Lanny's Roadhouse and Live Music Fridays and felt the panic rising again. He went into the living room with his coffee. The old lady, Alice, smiled at him. "So," she said, "you're with us another day."

"Yes. Unfortunate, a bit, for me, because I have a business deal in Toronto that I really should attend to."

"Oh well," said Alice. "Nothing's as urgent as it seems."

Lionel laughed. "Well. Sometimes it is. But I suppose in this case, it can wait."

"You see? It won't hurt you just to relax here for a day or two. Probably do you good. Get away from it all."

Lionel watched the falling snow. The coffee tasted good. The living room was warmer than upstairs. He wiggled his toes in his dry socks, the first he had worn in some twenty-four hours. He had had a good sleep; his vision seemed clearer, as if the bay window and the hooked rugs were outlined in fine pen lines.

He noticed the oil painting on the wall again, the dock and the boat loaded with lobster traps. All the shapes were filled with solid colour, and outlined with black. "I like that painting," he said, pointing. "Someone you know?"

"My mother," said the old lady softly. "Just after she had me. Would have been the late twenties."

"Really?" Lionel stood up to look at it closely. "Extraordinary."

"It's of the eastern shore, where we lived at the time."

Lionel looked at the lady more closely. She had a narrow, lined face, straight hair pulled tightly back. She would have been striking once. "Tell me," said Lionel, "were you there during the war?"

"No, dear, I was in Halifax for a little bit during the war, except for the time I was on a ship, and in Europe."

"Really? Because that's exactly why I asked, I was wondering if you had any contact with the convoys and — you were in Europe? Really?"

"And for some years after. In France."

"In France? Why in France?"

"Oh," she sighed, smiling, "it's a long story. *Hup.*" Her knitting needles clicked. "I went over with the British on D-day, and after the fighting ended —"

"Wait a minute," said Lionel, "you went over on *D-day?* What do you — I mean, what was a woman doing with the —"

"Well, not the exact D-day, I mean, not on the very first day, but a couple of days after. A week or so after. I was a reporter, with the BBC."

"A *reporter?* Really?"

"And I took photographs."

"Wow. *Wow.* Could I see some?"

Alice looked up at him with surprise. "If you really want to. Everyone here has seen them a million times."

"I *really* want to. Did you see action?"

"Oh yes, dear. Quite a bit, in France, and then in Holland. I had to be in a field hospital for a while in Holland because I got a bit of shrapnel in my leg. *Hyup.*" She went back to her knitting.

Lionel was silent. He stared at the old lady, then at the thick oil paint on the canvas of the lobster traps. He tried to picture her on the eastern shore of Nova Scotia — he didn't, actually, know which shore that was, but imagined it to be something like this shore, which he found, on later research trips, to be accurate — and then on the beaches of Normandy. He pictured her in a cotton-print dress in the thirties, in a town hall somewhere, and then in battle khaki, holding a camera. There was a whine of wind from outside.

"Still storming," she said, without looking out the window. She added faintly, "I had to go back, when they reached the Rhine, back to England." She paused, and even more faintly, said, "Because I was expecting."

"You were — Alice, hold on a minute, would you?" Lionel

stood up. "Just hold that for one second, don't forget what you were going to say, I'll be right back." He ran out of the room and tripped up the stairs, his socks slipping on the painted wood. He banged a shin and yelped and kept running. In his room he searched the pockets of his jacket, then of his other trousers. He searched every pocket of his bag, then dumped it out onto the bed and rummaged through his underwear. He did the same to the papers in his briefcase. He found a pen in there. Cursing, he slipped back down the stairs, to the coat rack in the front hall, where he finally found his notebook, in the inside pocket of his coat.

He slid back into the living room and sat down. "Okay," he said, flipping pages. "Now. Could we back up a bit? How did they let you onto the Normandy beaches, even a week after the invasion the fighting must have been pretty fierce, right? And I'm sure it wasn't easy for a woman —"

"Oh, it wasn't easy, that's for sure." She chuckled. "There were rules against it. That's why nobody knew I was a girl when I went over. I cut my hair, and there was this young lieutenant helped me get a uniform —"

"Holy mother of God," whispered Lionel. He was scribbling in his notebook. "Alice. You are extraordinary. You do know that, don't you? That you are extraordinary?"

"Oh, it wasn't extraordinary at the time, dear. You didn't think about it at the time. Nobody did."

Lionel wrote this down. He said, "You don't mind my taking notes, do you?" And then with more agitation, "Has anyone else interviewed you about this?"

"About what?"

"About your experiences in the war."

"Oh, there was a TV crew here, once, they were asking for reminiscences, you know, during the fiftieth anniversary."

"A local crew? Local CBC-TV?"

"I think that's what it was, yes."

Lionel waved them away. "Doesn't matter. Doesn't count. No other writers?"

"No, not a real writer. Would you like some more coffee?"

Lionel whistled. "Disguised as a man, ey? Now, let's back up a little further. How did you get from the eastern coast of Nova Scotia —"

"The eastern *shore*."

"To England?"

"Well. That's a long story."

Lionel put his sock feet up on a footstool. "I have all day, Alice. Possibly two days." They both laughed. "How about I make *you* some coffee?"

"No, thank you dear. Some tea would be nice."

An hour and a half later, Lionel was still writing. Alice had the photo album out. She was describing her childhood in Sheet Harbour, her father, the lobster fisherman, her mother, the arranger of church plays and frustrated artist, who would encourage young Alice to pursue her success in amateur theatricals all the way to Halifax. They were just getting to the first big trip to England, where a theatrical agent awaited her, when the phone rang.

"I'll get that," said Alice, rising slowly.

"No no. I'll get it." Lionel took his time getting to the black rotary-dial phone in the kitchen. His head was full. "Hello?"

"Lionel?"

"Sandra! How the hell did you find me here?"

"God *knows*, Lionel, it's been *hell*. Why didn't you call me, or your publisher, what's his name, we've been so worried about you, with the storm —"

"You heard about the storm?" said Lionel proudly.

"It's been on the national *news*, Li. I called Loon Lake and that guy —"

"Thalamus."

"He got me the number of the guy you were staying with, and I called there, and he said you'd gone off somewhere else, and —"

"No no. Just moved to another friend's house. Listen, I've just met the most incredible —"

"Li, how *are* you? Last time I spoke to you you were completely freaking out."

"Oh, you know." Lionel sighed. "Looks as if I'll be here another day. But you know. You take these things as they come."

"*What?*" Sandra began to laugh. "What did you say?"

"What do you mean?"

"Are you okay?"

"Yes, actually. I'm interviewing this woman, this old lady. The people here are quite interesting, actually."

"*What?* Who am I speaking to, please?"

"No, listen. Seriously. I have to keep my voice down. She's *incredible*, Deebee, she's had this most incredible life, reporter in the war, mother's this well-known folk artist, was an actress in London, then disguised herself, believe it or not, to get on shore at D-day, then had an affair with this French poet, this *resistance* fighter — I know, I know, it's *un*believable — and went back to Canada to have a baby, then came back *out* to France after the war to live with him, it just goes on and on, and I'm taking notes. And now here she is —"

"How do you know it's true?" Sandra said. She was a television producer.

"I've seen photographs. And now here she is, living completely unknown and unnoticed in this deserted port town on the East Coast. You know how *Lifelines* goes apeshit for this true-to-life stuff. I'm thinking a novella, I'm thinking movie of the week, you know, based on a true story, you know, Michiyo can give this to Franco Goseiwicz, he'd go wild for something that —"

"Goseiwicz?" said Sandra. "I thought you wouldn't go near him."

"Oh well." Lionel shrugged. "You never know. We'll see what happens."

"Lionel, you are just frighteningly laid-back. What happened with Pyramid? Have you contacted Michiyo?"

He sighed again. The snow was stopping, a moon-like sunlight glowing on the blanket, as if filtered through gauze. "No."

"Why not? Have you heard the news about —"

"I don't want to hear it. I don't want to know about what's going on with Pyramid, Deeb, honestly, I don't. I can't explain it. It's just not good for me to worry about that stuff. "

"Well, I've always thought so too."

There was a silence. Lionel looked through the glittering window. "I might even stay here, if they let me, which I'm sure they will, because they've been incredibly nice to me, and write a bit on this. It's funny, Alice mentioned a bar which was the first bar ever in Halifax, which they closed on V-E Day, because they were afraid of riots, which led to riots, which is amusing, anyway, it turns out I've actually been in that bar, I was just there the day after I flew in, and there was something about it that really charmed me. Anyway. You're probably not interested."

"No. Tell me."

"Well, in fact, it's funny, I was just thinking about that bar, yesterday, it has these ancient trestle tables with initials carved in them, and these massive Celtic waiters with red beards —"

"Really? Honestly *red* beards?"

"Honestly, truly red. It just seems totally unchanged since the war. I can really picture Alice in it. Although women probably weren't allowed. I'll have to find out. But there were all these young kids there embracing each other, I think it was a Christmas thing, I think they were all home from away, as they say. There was this sense of funny, I don't know, pride, about this run-down old place, which I've never felt, you know, because we moved around so much as kids, after Italy and England, and then Prague, and I guess I've never felt . . . I don't know."

"What?"

"It would be interesting to imagine if you were actually *from* here."

"Why from there?"

"From anywhere, really. It would be interesting to imagine being from somewhere, you know, really *from* somewhere. Which I am not."

Sandra laughed softly. "It sounds highly unusual. No, I mean it, it sounds great. But it means you're not coming home right away?"

"Would you like me to?"

"Yes."

Lionel put his fingers against the glass, felt its cold. "So why did you call me, anyway? I thought you didn't want to talk."

"Well, you sounded so sad yesterday. I was worried about you."

Lionel felt his chest expanding again with the expensive feeling, the warm liquid feeling. "Thanks, Deebee. You're nice. I'm sorry about all my bullshit."

"Lionel."

"Yes?"

"You haven't called me that for a long time."

He paused. "No. Do you mind?"

She laughed. "No. I can get used to it. Again."

"I'm glad. I'm *really* glad. Deebee." They laughed together.

"When are you coming home?"

"Well, maybe tomorrow. Maybe the next day. I'll call you when I know."

"Lionel, you know I can't live that way. I'm busy this week, I have two ten-minute documentary sections we're finishing —"

"Hey," said Lionel, "hey, relax. I'll let you know, as soon as I know. Listen. This is good."

"Okay. Good. Okay."

"I'm going to see you soon."

"I know." She giggled. "Why are you being so romantic? It's not like you."

"I don't know. Look, I've got to get back to this interview. I'm really excited about this. And I have this idea for a story, maybe a Christmas story, that I might be able to get to *Edge* in time to make up for the piece they . . . anyway, even if it doesn't get in, I want to go back to this bar. I want to imagine what it's like to be from here."

"That's good," said Sandra. "That's great. It's good to hear you excited again."

"What about you? Are you fine?"

"Yes. I'm fine."

"Glad to hear it."

"Okay. I'm hanging up now. I'll see you soon. You're sure you're okay?"

"*Hyup*," said Lionel, in an intake of breath. He took a sip of his hot tea. A circle of stained glass hung by a string in the window, twirling slowly and catching the pale light. "*Hyup*."

When he went back into the living room, Alice said, "I was telling you about when they tried to close the liquor stores. My word, that was a sight."

Lionel took up his notebook. "Tell me," he said.

Home

What you have to do is escape your family.

You've been back a couple of days and you've already been up and down the shopping street twice, ducking your head against the wet wind from the harbour, you've looked in the food court at the great salmon pink faux-marble mall for people you might recognize from high school, you've had a coffee in the Second Cup on the corner, watching the row of people of indeterminate age in team jackets and baseball caps with all their belongings in plastic bags, waiting outside the Lord Nelson in the snow for the bus to Herring Cove. Other than this there is the TV in your parents' basement with TSN and the unbelievably bright football fields of Southern states.

But the last Friday before Christmas, the last Friday before the radio silence of church and family meals, is the night to go downtown. You run almost all the way, sliding wherever possible on snow. You slide all the way down the steep hill of Blowers to Argyle, to the green wooden door under the hanging wooden sign.

You push open the door and look down the stairs and you hear the noise and feel the heat already rising: you have to walk carefully down these stairs, straight towards two men sitting on stools at the bottom, watching you closely for signs of threat, their arms folded and bulging. You just have to walk past them.

The room is brightly lit, low ceilinged, furnished with long trestle tables scarred with initials. It is so packed you hesitate for a moment. One of the big red-haired waiters sits at the threshold with a massive tray of draft glasses already filled and foamy. It is too jammed for the waiter to circulate with such a weight inside; it's easier for you to buy a bunch here and come back when you need more, which is fine, because you are suddenly seized with an overwhelming thirst. You have pulled out your wallet and asked for two to start, but Ted and Jimmy are already there, yelling and clapping you on the back and paying: they hand you four and you have to follow them into the fray, spilling.

The music is pounding, muffled: the speakers still have not been fixed. The people look the same: there are the black boots and leather jackets of the art college students and the brown workboots and baseball caps of the guys with jobs or between them, but you don't recognize many of them, especially the women, even the one with the wild hair and the black choker who appears to be looking at you and who may be the one who went out with Claude and played in that band.

In fact, you notice that many of them are looking at you and that they are extremely young and this frightens you and excites you, as this place always has done; you feel your face getting hot, especially since the first two draft went down so quickly. The music in the air is like invisible sex and everything is aggressive. People are bumping you and spilling your beer and you want to look everywhere at once.

Across the room you see Richard McCormack and Andy Boutilier and everybody is yelling "HOW YA DOIN'" and crushing your hand and you are quickly down to the serious business of yelling in Ted's ear, "Now, Ted, tell me, who is that person over there, in the black dress?"

Hoarsely, he yells, "That blonde person? In the black dress? That's Donny MacDonald's little sister."

And you yell, "NO! Not his *littlest* sister?"

"Come a long way, hasn't she?"

"Really, eh? Now who does she go out with now?"

"She married Donny MacKenzie."

"No!"

You can talk like this for some time. You are vaguely aware of your accent changing as you speak. You kiss Blythe McCracken on the cheek and notice that she is looking older and unfortunately like an elementary schoolteacher, which is what she is, and you wonder why you used to be so painfully in love with her. You and Ted buy each other four more draft, and you see the girl with the choker again: she has dark red lips and huge dark eyes and she wears something incredible, a shining silver T-shirt which appears to be made of rubber or at least spandex and apparently nothing underneath. It makes you shiver. And she doesn't took too young either, maybe twenty-five; she's maybe even doing an MFA, which is good and bad — she sees you looking at her and you smile but her face is impassive; she turns away.

Suddenly it is very bright in here, and you are coughing with the smoke and you feel a little sick. You walk as carefully as you can to the heavy wooden door of the men's. A row of guys is lined up at the urinals, leaning their heads against the wall. The flaps on their caps are flattened against their heads as padding.

You take your place and the guy next to you, a little guy with a moustache and a cap that reads, "STEELES PACKING PRODUCTS" or "AGGRESSIVE TUBE BENDING," says to you without turning his head, "Time to turn in the rental, eh?"

You say, "Seriously. You don't buy it, you only rent it," and you both laugh.

He says, "You see they took the murals down though, eh?"

You say, "Is that right?" trying to remember the murals.

"Yup. Owners did. Fuckm found out they were too fuckm valuable, and soldm. You can see the white spots on the walls."

"Right. Noticed that."

"I guess they were worth fuckm all kinds of coin."

"Is that right?"

After you come out you spend a long time watching the tight jeans of a woman playing pool, arched and taut over the edge of the table, and asking the Bog about the younger sisters of friends; in fact, you don't know how much time has passed, but suddenly it must be closing time, because the music has stopped and the bright lights have come on and there is a hammering: the big, mustachioed, red-haired waiters are slamming bottles on tables to get your attention, bellowing, "OKAY, PEOPLE, TIME TO GO!"

There is a groaning and muttering. You almost trip over a bottle. Bang bang bang bang. "LET'S GO, PEOPLE!"

There is broken glass underfoot, a vague uneasiness in the shifting crowd in the brightness. There is something needed to finish this; not enough has happened yet.

You start to move towards the door but there is a commotion near the bar, a swirling of jackets. A knot of jackets is grappling, heads down, reeling around in a wide arc, knocking glasses off tables. Two guys in Gore-tex, each with the other in a headlock. You can't see who it is. A roar goes up, and the gleeful crowd, girls and boys alike, forms a circle. Who is it? You can't see! Ted screams with delight, "It's Darryl! Darryl MacInnis and some little guy! Oh my Jesus!"

You stand on a chair to watch, your heart pounding, in time to see the great red-haired monolithic waiters pull them apart like rags, and are rushing them up the stairs to the street, muttering, "Take it outside, boys."

You all follow to see the end. Now this is Christmas. It has been snowing again; you can't tell if the crunching under your feet is new snow or broken glass. There is a crowd outside every bar, up and down the street. Darryl and the little guy, who now appears to be Jamie McQuarrie the son of the head of neurosurgery and who is now at fucking Princeton or some fucking thing, have thrown a couple of half-hearted punches and are degenerating into wrestling again, but that subsides too, and before you know it they're following their friends off to the Moon, which is open till three.

The Bog is waggling his head and saying, "Darryl McInnis. Oh my Jesus," over and over again, and you laugh but your hands are shaking. Something flashes in the corner of your eye and you turn to see the silver T-shirt and the wild black hair like a great shining spider of the art college girl: she's laughing with her friends. Her jacket is open and her lips are still incredibly dark, black in the lamplight, which makes you sad until you realize that she is smiling at you. Her mouth is open and her teeth are white and she is smiling. You smile back, and then she is dancing off down the street with her friends who are making a lot of noise.

Jimmy is asking you something and you say, "Sure, sure, the Palace or the Moon, wherever." You suck on the icy air and listen to the noises echoing from all over the downtown, the distant whoops and screams and tires spinning on ice. You look up at the flakes glittering metallic in the streetlight like teeth, and for that second you are scared again and very, very happy.

JAMES

Responsibility

■

"Perhaps you don't value it now, but as you get older money becomes more important," said his mother. She was sitting in the breakfast nook with her tea, looking out at the bird feeder. James too was looking out at the garden, standing at the sliding doors. Anyone who talked in the kitchen did so while looking at the garden.

"I'm sure that's true, but you see, believe it or not, I'm hoping to make money from my writing, eventually. I know that seems ridiculous to you and Dad." He waited for her to contradict him. "Some people actually make a great deal of money from what I . . . the kind of writing I'm trying to do. I'm talking to some people about a documentary, about my music column, it could be a book, it could . . ." He clenched his jaw shut. He felt helpless. "It could be the kind of book that would sell outside this little . . . anyway. Yes, it's a bigger risk, yes, but actually it could pay off very well, if you do something successful. So actually I'm being *more* ambitious than you and Dad were."

"I guess it's just the risk I worry about."

It was no longer surprising that this conversation came up, even that it came up on the Sunday afternoons of his visits, that it came up just as simultaneous relief and tension about the trip back to the city were growing with a mental hum, ripening in him, in his nervous and circulatory systems like some slowly developing and ultimately convulsive disease, just as they were all about to begin the bargaining about which parent in which car would drive him to the bus station and dump him in its stained limbo air and promise of metamorphosis, this was so familiar it was no longer surprising; what was surprising was how unfailingly and deeply it seared him with a fine painful clear sense of abandonment, as would some long penetrating parental angioscopic device, every time, and made him think, every time, that perhaps now, this time, was the time it would all come out, it would come clear exactly what it was about what he did that so disappointed her, and why her disappointment so irritated — no, worse, let's be honest — so hurt him. He said quickly, "And you worry about my lifestyle, that I'm not married and —"

"I don't care that you're not married, if you're happy."

"Yes you do. Don't pretend you don't. Of course you do. You'd like me to be married and have kids and a minivan and come over on Sundays and talk about eavestroughing with Dad."

"*I* don't think you could *handle* kids," said his mother with the restrained tone of someone producing an ace.

"No, I couldn't," said James.

She was silent for a moment. Then she said, "But when you do have children, you'll want to be able to provide for them, and I think you should think of that now."

He turned to her and said gently, "Mom, what would you say

if I told you I might never have children? Do you think there's something wrong with that?"

She was silent again. She twirled a strand of hair around a finger, which meant that she was agitated. She would never sit down for so long in mid-morning unless she was upset. The tea in her cup was getting cold.

"You think that's somehow morally wrong, not to have children, don't you?" said James. He felt merciless; he felt this was the time to get it all out.

"No," she said quickly, "not at all. It's you I'm thinking of. I just think that you would be happier with children. Having children . . . it takes you out of yourself. You would stop chasing after every girl you met and —"

"What if I don't want to stop chasing after every girl I meet? You seem to feel that I have to at a certain point, because everybody does. Why? What if it makes me happy?"

"It won't make you happy forever."

"Will children?"

She was silent again. "Look, all I know is that all this tension in your life, all that awful time you had with Alison and that girl in the city when they wouldn't speak to each other and —"

"Yes," said James, "I know, go on."

"All that wouldn't happen if you had a family. You wouldn't have time for it. And all I know is that when you have a child, that's the most important thing. If your child is happy, then you're happy, it's as simple as that. And you're — what is it that Joanne Winterson always said? You're only as happy as your most unhappy child. It's true." She took quick sips at her tea, which by now was surely cold.

"Sounds terrific." He puffed out his cheeks. "Just remind me again why this is a better system?"

"Oh, don't be so snooty. You're so *arrogant*."

"What? Sorry. I'm not following you."

"Yes you are. You know exactly what I mean. You're so condescending."

James turned back to the garden. "I have no idea what you're talking about." But he did. He made an effort to make an effort to think about trying to be nicer. He said, "I don't mean to be nasty about anyone's choices. As long as you *make* choices."

"What about Jennifer? Doesn't she want children?"

James took a deep breath. "Well, not right now she doesn't. She's trying to get her own career going, she's in the same boat as me. We have more . . ." He stopped himself. He said, "She's just too busy, and she doesn't have the money or the stability in her life for it. She doesn't want kids right now."

"Well, she's over thirty now. She doesn't have much time left."

"So maybe she won't. Maybe she won't have time. I'm not sure, because we haven't talked about it a lot, but I think that right now at least she isn't too worried about it. She's thinking about herself, about her career. Like me."

"*Oh!* But. . ." His mother leaned over the table to pour more tea. She spilled the tea and said, "*Bother*." She was frowning and biting her lip; she really was agitated and maybe about to cry. He wasn't sure what it was all about and he got agitated too. He handed her a cloth. At least they were getting somewhere.

"But what?" He sat down at the table.

She wiped the table with furious speed. "What she wants, what you want," she said, shaking her head. "You people — it's always what *you* want. You just think you can play around and have fun forever."

"Yes. Perhaps we do. What should we do instead?" His heart was beating fast.

She didn't answer.

"What is it, exactly, Mom, that upsets you? That I don't have enough responsibilities in life? Is that it?"

There was a long silence and then she said in a faint voice, "Yes."

"I have too much fun. I don't have enough to tie me down."

"James, if your father and I had felt like you," she said urgently, looking at him, "then you wouldn't even *be* here!"

"Right." James rubbed his face with his hands. "The logic of this is growing too much for me." He sighed. "Mom. You don't understand what I'm . . . Look at it this way. Imagine you had never had me. Or Kurt. Then you wouldn't, you wouldn't feel a responsibility to us, right? Because we wouldn't —"

"I can't imagine that," she said in a higher voice, her indignant voice. "Lucky for you, I couldn't imagine that."

"That's my point, Mom. That you're not imagining what I'm —"

"You think," she said rapidly, "that you can just live this student life forever, have no —"

"Why not? Why can't I —"

"But it's not all fun. At a certain point you have to pay the piper. At a certain point you just have to stop fooling around and accept your responsibilities."

James looked at her. She was fidgeting with a doily. "What responsibilities? My family responsibilities?"

"*Yes.*"

"Mom, this is what I'm trying to get at. Think about it. If I don't have a wife or kids then who do I have a responsibility to?"

There was a long silence. She was fingering the doily on the tray that held the salt and pepper shakers and the bowl of sugar and the tiny antique silver spoons from the ancestral Germany that was unknown to them all, moving her eyes from the doily out to the bird feeder where there were no birds and back again.

"What is it?" he said more gently. "Is it that you think I have a responsibility to Jennifer, or maybe to you?"

"No, no, not to me, certainly."

"Is it just that you feel I have a responsibility to *have* kids? So that I can feel a responsibility to them? This is what I mean about logical —"

"No, no, I'm not saying that. I'm not saying you *have* to."

He waited. She did not go on. "I don't have to."

"No."

"Okay, so what — why —"

"I don't know." Her voice sounded weak now. "I'm not sure. I'm not sure — I don't know what I mean." She played with the doily.

James thought about this. He looked at the doily, which she had inherited from her mother who had crocheted in it Portage la Prairie, a place he had never been, and wondered for some reason how old she had been when it had been crocheted. He had a black-and-white picture of his mother in a rather Chanel-like tweed suit, leaning against the hood of a large American car, against an unblemished sky and a flat wheaty horizon of laughably pure rural nowhere. He wondered how old she had been in that photograph; probably younger, yes, much younger than him. "Are you saying, Mom, maybe that . . . maybe it's just that you, when you were young, I mean younger, you felt you didn't . . ." He stopped himself. He wanted to say, *You didn't have a choice.*

"Oh, we didn't even think about it. Everyone had children. It was all — it was what we wanted."

"Right." He paused. He had to go very carefully here. "But have you ever thought about how, about how things might have . . . about what you might have done if you hadn't" — he took a deep breath — "had me and Kurt."

She stood up abruptly and stood in the window, while James thought, She never does that, never takes a moment to stare at the garden without a vacuum cleaner or a duster in her hand. Her arms were folded and her shoulders hunched. She said, "You sound as if you *want* me to think about that."

"No." He didn't know what she was getting at, but the safe answer was no. "No, no. I just, I'm thinking of me, in my case —"

"If I hadn't got married? Is that what you mean?"

"I don't know. Was it impossible to get married and not have children? Not that I'm saying that's what you should —"

"Well, I suppose it wasn't impossible. But I wanted children. Your dad wanted children. And, you know, Jamie" — she gave a small laugh — "I was very flattered, you know, that Hans wanted to marry me. He was, I knew he was going to be very successful. You didn't turn down opportunity, in those days."

James laughed, too. As the refrigerator began to hum unevenly, he became aware of a cloud of worry too vague to describe, forming over his head. "It meant your problems were solved."

"Sure. And he wanted children too, you know, it wasn't just my idea."

"Yes. Okay. But what, I guess I mean to ask, what if you hadn't got married?"

"I suppose I would have had to get some kind of job."

James asked slowly, "Did you want . . . to do that?"

"No. I suppose not." She paused. "I don't know."

He held himself very still. Her voice had gone small as she had said it. His worry buzzed and shifted overhead. He didn't know what was approaching them here, but it was something grey and tight. He thought of the bus station, its cigarette air.

"I guess you don't respect at all what I did," she said in a wavering voice. "Bringing you two boys up."

"Of course I do, Mom. Of course I do. I know how much work it is, how hard —"

"No you don't."

It was James's turn to be silent.

She said, in a voice that fluttered and broke, "There was a time when people thought it was valuable, to run a house and sew and clean and cook for two boys and a man, and educate the boys, the way I read to you —"

"Mom," said James, agitated, "of course I value that. Of course I respect —"

"No you don't. You don't think it meant — it's not important to you. You think if it's not some big career it's not difficult and it's, it's some kind of cop-out."

"No," said James.

"I've heard you say it. When you found out Alison had a child you said it was a cop-out."

James opened his mouth and closed it. It was true, not only that he had said it, but that he believed it. It was a cop-out.

"The work of about twenty-two years. A cop-out."

He looked at the doily, her moving hands.

"And you're not the only one," she said quietly. "I can tell people laugh at me. The younger wives at Dad's firm."

James went cold. "No they don't. They wouldn't."

"They think we're ridiculous, me and Joanne and . . . all of my friends. I can tell. And maybe they're right."

"Oh, Mom, don't be —"

"You know, Jamie, I was thinking about this last week. I was trying to remember all the jobs I've had in my life. All the paying jobs." She counted on her fingers. "I used to babysit, as a teenager. I must have earned less than a dollar an hour. And I was in a nursing course when I met Dad, but I worked in an office in the summers. So that was two summers, about four months' total. And then I worked at the kindergarten, where you and Kurt went, for about two years, part-time, for a little extra cash, when we were just starting out."

James listened to the anxious fridge.

"So," she said, "I counted it all up. All the money I've ever earned. Myself. And I figured it came to a total of about three thousand five hundred dollars. In my whole life. That's all I've ever earned myself. I never thought about it, until now. I guess, I guess that's all the young women see. The other things we did, what we did, it's not important to anyone any more. I guess."

The refrigerator grunted, shuddered and stopped humming. The kitchen was silent.

He said as gently as he could, "Yes it is, Mom. I don't think the money's important. I do think it was a disappointing choice for Alison, because she had her music, and her . . ." He trailed off. He did not want to imply that his mother had had nothing else to do.

But it was true. "She gave up her music. But you, there were fewer opportunities at that —"

"And I didn't have anything I could have done? Is that what you mean? And Alison shouldn't have done the most important thing in the world?" She balled her little hand into a fist and made to punch his shoulder, but of course she didn't. "You're all so selfish." Her voice wavered again.

"What?" said James, alarmed. "Who is? Alison?"

"It's just that . . . you're all so arrogant about everything. It's just not very . . . it's not very *nice*." Her voice cracked and he realized she was in tears.

He stood behind her and put a hand on her shoulder. His worry was gone, and in its place he had a pure, liquid anguish, a sense that the air itself was sad, over the silent garden, that forces were moving all around him like invisible rain. He said, "What isn't nice, Mom? Tell me."

"I can't explain it. It's just that . . ." She sniffled. "Nice people . . ." She paused and coughed. Then she said, loud and cracking, as if in physical distress, "*Nice people don't do things for themselves.*"

She was really sobbing.

He felt as if the floor of his stomach had opened, and there was darkness below it.

He patted her shoulder. She sobbed and shook. There was nothing else to do but pat her shoulder. He looked around the immaculate kitchen, the slate-tiled floor, the island and the overhead wrought-iron pot hooks she had campaigned so hard to have his father put in. The sandy wall, the pristine counters. The pot lids were stacked in the pot-lid rack; the utensils hung from hooks over the island. "I'm sorry, Mom," he said. "*You're* nice."

He tried a laugh and she giggled, too, a sniffling giggle as if she was embarrassed, and wiped her eyes and blew her nose. He exhaled in relief, for if she was blowing her nose already, the whole thing was okay. He glanced at his watch: there was a bus back to the city at 3:15.

He put his arm around her shoulder and they looked at the empty garden, the wrought-iron chairs. He wondered what she was going to do that afternoon, after he got back on his bus. His dad had had to go into the office. And Kurt was gone, probably gone for good now, even when he got back from Whistler he would be looking for a job in the city. James wondered for a second if he should stay, maybe take her out to the craft shops. He thought of the drive through the industrial park, the deserted highways, the hot little shops. He thought of the hand-made towel racks and calico quilts and apple dolls they would look at. The photo frames in amusing shapes. If they drove out of town, they would have to stop and buy corn and squash, for it was that time, which would go into soups and preserves and pie fillings which only his dad would eat.

He stared at the garden. There were no birds at the bird feeder. The house was dead quiet; the whole neighbourhood was silent as a tomb. And he knew then that he wasn't nice, he wasn't a nice person, because all he wanted to do was get out, get the hell out of there.

Team
Canada

■

James was startled by the utter dark at a quarter after five, outside the Eaton Centre. Night fell: whoomp. He'd only just left the house; he thought he'd have another two hours of light, of shopping, get it all done. The temperature dropped by five degrees with an almost audible whine, as thermometers dove like bombs all over the city. He could feel warmth hissing out from the top of his head, warmth draining from the soles of his feet and his naked palms, a great sluice of escaping heat. He stood in the crowd of charcoal coats waiting to board the streetcar. He forgot where he was going next. People, apparently having heard the sirens too, began to move more quickly, rushing past him with a new determination, new frowns. They were all turning up their collars, staring at the sidewalks, now grey as something burnt in the fluorescence. The streetcar gave off white light. There was an urgency in the boarding of it.

Wind seared his cheek and pierced his unbuttoned overcoat and he cursed, turning his back to it. He fumbled for gloves in the pocket with the holes, dropping his shopping bag.

He had bought one present, he could tell himself that, two CDs for his father as usual, but that had been easy ("The Marching Band of the Black and Tans Live at the Glasgow Tattoo," plus a remastering of "The Best of Don Messer's Singalong Jubilee" — a slightly more penetrating choice than last year's Tony Bennett/Glen Miller/The Royal Canadian Air Farce Live on Parliament Hill combination, which had nevertheless been massively, heartbreakingly successful), and he was already late for Jennifer and he only had another hour before the shops all closed, to think of something beautiful and sensual but not too overtly sexy so she didn't take it as a hint (which it was) and bring up the whole "you're not satisfied with our sex life" discussion again.

He had carefully avoided the lingerie shops in the mall, glimpsing purple silk and straps out of the corner of his eye. He had concentrated instead on the heroic, big-eyed effort required to propel his body in a vaguely forward direction through the morass of shuffling, gaping, bag-laden mall bodies. Further distraction arose from his growing consciousness that all the Italian and Portuguese girls seemed suddenly to be wearing the same skintight, snake-like shiny black stretchy trousers, all around him.

A woman had banged him with an enormous box marked "Humidifier and Water Purifier," then scuttled off, staggering under its weight. He had actually considered it for a minute, impressed by people's inventiveness. Who would think of humidifiers at a time like this, with all the displays bursting with garters and cleavage? But he did actually consider it. Not very romantic, but perhaps she had complained once of dry skin? Or perhaps it was damp.

He had managed to pass the fake English pubs, his throat immediately parched. The bars were crammed with laughing guys in suits who presumably had finished their shopping or who, braver than James, simply didn't care. Their strong hands around fat pints of beer, glowing wheat-coloured.

He put on his gloves and buttoned his coat and squinted against the wind and tried to concentrate. A tall Italian woman with red lips strode through the crowd with a confidence so towering it seemed like scorn. He noticed her suede shoes as they disappeared.

Did Italian women in navy or purple suede shoes ever worry about water purity? He shook his head. He remembered he had been thinking about a book, something artistic, something lush with perhaps nudes in it which she wouldn't immediately recognize as sexual. And there was an art bookstore just west along Queen, which would entail a bitter walk but which would necessitate passing Mirage, where David might be working the bar, and Control, which had recently added an oyster bar which James, as an occasional restaurant critic for *Edge* magazine, felt professionally compelled to check out, even if only for a very quick beer, which was all he had time for and indeed all he wanted (and which, further in its favour, would be write-offable as a research expense).

He began walking, promising himself that he would enter Mirage only if in fact it was David behind the bar, as it was only friendly to say hello, when he remembered that bloody message from his editor.

He stopped still, and suddenly intensely hated the grinding streetcar, the hideous belted overcoat and plastic shopping bags of the man in front of him, *all* belted overcoats, the numbingly ugly massive concrete upturned flying saucer of the city hall, now illuminated like a great monument to outdated futuristic sixties architecture; he cursed with plague and oblivion all failed futuristic utopian visions everywhere, all concrete; he condemned the pitiful little skating rink and its institutional neon glow, he damned to eternal suffering all cheerful cute skaters, all pom-pommed hats, all graceful athletic thugs with Team Canada jerseys, all idiotically happy normal people who owned skates everywhere, all cold fingertips, all frozen toes; he cursed the cold and he hated the cold, he hated the cold and he hated the cold, and he hated himself for not remembering to return Julian's call which, earlier in the day, had sounded urgent.

He put his head down and ran against the wind to a phone booth on the corner of University. He had to remove his gloves to hold the quarter, which he dropped onto the ice. And since he couldn't find it again and had no other quarter, he had to find his calling card and pay $1.50 to call an office about three blocks away.

"*Edge* MA-gazine, please *hold*," sang the receptionist, and muted him.

James sang, "Please fuck *off*," along with the Muzak. It was a synthesized version of "Jingle Bell Rock." He tried to breathe deeply and regularly. He visualized a beer glowing like a sun, the misted glass, his hand on it. He wiggled his toes in his shoes. He traced the word *asshole* in his breath on the glass with his numb finger.

"*Edge* MA-gazine," she shouted again, "sorry to keep you —"

"Julian please," snapped James, "it's James Willing."

"One *mo*-ment."

Radio limbo again.

"Jingle bell, jingle bell, jingle bell rock," sang James. He hopped from foot to foot, looking at his watch. "Fuck jingle-bell-fuck, fuck jingle-bell-fuck." It was probably some little fact-checking problem with the piece on specialty hairdressers, or a small cut, something he could fix over the phone. He prayed it wasn't a new assignment. He couldn't do it. For once, he would be strong and tell Julian he didn't need the money, he wouldn't take any more last-minute —

"James!" said Julian. "James." Julian savoured everyone's name like this, as if in marvel at the felicity of it, as if he could have asked for nothing better of his day than some serendipitous contact with this person. James could picture his clean hair, his Japanese linen shirt, his heavy shoes up on the desk. It exhausted him.

"Hi Julian," he said weakly, "you're working late."

"A little," said Julian. "We have a bit of a crisis here. I tried to call you earlier."

James felt a coldness in his belly. "Sorry. I've been busy. Is it a problem with the fact-checking on the hairdressers' thing?"

"No, no, that's fine. Actually, it's — listen, do you have any time this week? It's kind of urgent and I was thinking it might be up your alley."

"This *week*?" James opened his mouth and gave a soundless scream. "Let me guess. You need something written, right? A whole new piece, right? And don't tell me, it's for December, right?"

"Right. Which is now a month and a half past its regular deadline. Which means things are rather tense around here."

"Jesus Christ." James leaned into the glass wall of the booth. A man in a trenchcoat was waiting outside, his shoulders hunched against the wind. James closed his eyes and tried to picture Julian's glass-partitioned cubicle, its corkboard papered with fashion stills, the portrait of Le Corbusier, the solemn photograph of a Charles Eames chair. Julian would be casually watching the art department through the glass, all the long skirts and chunky boots. "Jesus

Christ. I can't, Julian, I'm sorry, I — what the hell happened? Did something fall through?"

Julian laughed shortly. "You could say something fell through. The Lionel Baratelli fiction. You remember we were going to run some fiction, some Christmas fiction?"

"The Baratelli fell — Jesus, that was two thousand words long. You mean you've got a hole two thousand words long?"

"Right in the middle of the book. The pages were already laid out. We've got Christmas illustrations and everything. Beautiful ones. Juanita Love did them."

"Cool," said James, impressed. He had a brief vision of Juanita Love in the snake costume she had posed in for *Random*. He tried not to think of convincing Jennifer to try on a snake costume. "You must have paid her a wad."

"Yes," said Julian crisply. "Yes we did, and now we're going to find some goddam way of using them."

"What happened with the piece? He didn't come through? Or" — James smiled grimly to himself — "or was it just too sentimental? Although what you expect from writers like Lionel Baratelli I can't imagine. Was it about a sad, slow divorce?"

"Now, James —"

"Or a sad story about a middle-aged writer who can't write . . . and a dog dying. Or an old lady. Or a horse. Or perhaps —"

"Okay James, cool it."

"Perhaps the problem was that he was just too old. Is that it? You guys finally realized, hey, *I* know, you all said, *I* know what the problem is, this guy's too *old!*"

Julian grudged him a sharp exhalation that may have been a laugh. "All right. Stop. You'll be pleased to know it was none of the above. He came through all right. With a clever little story about a politician who bears a close resemblance to the mayor. He was in his bitter mode. I thought it was great. Good and nasty. Very funny. I didn't think of getting it lawyered until about a week ago. I thought maybe there may be some small problem we could fix by changing names or . . . anyway. They freaked out. Said it's completely libellous from beginning to end. Then it got leaked, and then we got some particularly scary letters from Milovac's own lawyer, and anyway, Robertson freaked out, and the whole thing is canned. It can't be saved."

James paused a moment. His mouth was dry. He couldn't resist; he asked, "So what do you need?"

"Well," said Julian, "nothing that would need a lot of research. Something personal and Christmassy."

"I've never done fiction before in my life."

"Well, it wouldn't be exactly fiction. More like a memoir. Something funny and nasty, snarky. You do snarky so well, and we're low on snarky in this issue. But uplifting. A story or like a reminiscence with a Christmas message, like you have to learn something, or something. Try to describe some time when you learned something about Christmas."

James laughed. The man outside was frowning at him and tapping on his watch. Eight lanes of traffic on University Avenue were roaring past with the sound of a gale. "Snarky but uplifting. Right."

"Right. Listen, I know it's short notice, but —"

"Julian, I am *so* busy this week. I have two restaurant reviews, a profile, I have parties out the yingyang, my girlfriend is — I haven't done *any* of my shopping and I have to *go away* on Friday to this goddam conference that I personally couldn't —"

"James, it would pay well."

"How well?"

"Two thousand words, two thousand bucks. And no research, right? And let's say twenty-two hundred. Twenty-four hundred, because it's such short notice. I need you, James. Help me out."

James was silent. His mouth was dry. He looked at his watch: he was going to be late for Jennifer. He thought of the coming week, his promises to her. This was the week they were really going to spend time together and work things out and not always be so rushed. If he worked, it would mean one hell of a loving present. He thought of all the lingerie stores and the books bulging with fleshy nudes and he felt exhausted. He thought of the two letters from VISA lying unopened on his desk.

"All right." He looked at his watch again. "But more than a week. I need two weeks."

Julian was silent for a second. "A week and a half."

James looked up at the flashing weather beacon on top of the Canada Life building: descending white rings: temperature dropping. "A week and a half." He twisted his neck the other way and looked up, way up the concrete tower to the top a kilometre up, its lights flashing in the sky and the invisible restaurant slowly revolving above them, a great concrete block frozen up there in the blue-black air.

She would probably have opened the wine already, and may be grimly drinking it in her kitchen, in the apartment where he was invited for dinner and probably would stay over, as he had done the night before last, again provoking mutual but tacit consideration of why he wasn't just getting on with it and moving in already. A question which could not, much as he would like to evade it, be infinitely delayed. If he spent the week working, he would have to refuse the visit to her parents in Aurora. He laughed, filled with a sort of desperate glee. "Sure. Why not. Why the fuck not." He sighed. "I'll call you tomorrow when I have some ideas."

He stepped out of the phone booth. While the angry guy fumbled with his own coins, James breathed deeply, considered the next phone call, and his explanation. The money angle would be good. He tried to remember a Christmas story which had happened to him and couldn't remember anything but the time he had seen Mrs. Harris slap Mr. Harris in the kitchen at his parents' eggnog party. He felt ill.

He waited for a long time in the cold, watching the white temperature rings dancing downwards on the tower. When his turn came he had to use his calling card again.

She answered quickly. "Hello?"

"Hi, it's me, sorry. Look, I'm sorry, I'm going to be just a little late. Something really a big fucking drag —"

"Jamie!" Her voice was warm, eager. She never called him that. "It's *okay*."

"Oh. Good." He paused. "It's just another piece for . . ." He trailed off. "Are you okay?"

There was a long moment of silence, in which he thought for a second that he heard, behind the grunt of buses, a sniffle. "Jenny! What's wrong?"

"Nothing," she said in a choked voice. "Nothing at all." And then she giggled, a crying giggle, and blew her nose. "I can't wait to see you."

"Jenny!" His heart was accelerating. "What is it? What's wrong?"

"Nothing. Just something good happened. It's silly." She was laughing and sniffling and sputtering. "It's kind of embarrassing."

There was something so ridiculous about the blowing and sputtering that James found himself laughing, too.

"James?"

"Yes."

"It's so weird."

"*What?*" He tried to keep his voice even.

"I was just waiting for you, and I have such a nice dinner ready, I have a salmon trout that I stuffed with —"

"Yes," said James, "come on, Jenny, this is killing me."

"And I had some wine open and I had a glass and you still weren't here so I had another one. And then I got sleepy and I went in the bedroom and I was lying on the bed and reading the Victoria's Secret catalogue, just because it was there."

"Uh huh," said James, guiltily, because he had left it there.

"And I was just looking at all the beautiful bodies and all those bras and tiny little G-strings and stuff and I started to get, you know."

James began to smile.

"It's kind of weird, I guess."

"No," said James quickly, "it's not weird at all."

"For once it didn't bug me, it didn't seem like a big deal, is all. I guess I was imagining wearing all that lacy stuff and being beautiful and —"

"You are beautiful," he said gently.

"And anyway, I thought of that silk teddy you got me that I never wear." She paused.

James felt a brief pain.

"And I — I don't know why but I got it out and it really is beautiful, you know, it's a gorgeous colour and I'm sorry I never wear it."

James cleared his throat.

"And I took off all my clothes and I put it on and it felt really soft and, so, I got into bed and it was so warm and . . . I started to, you know." She laughed high and clear.

"Yes." James was grinning. Under his coat and wool, his body was reacting.

"And I never do that, but it just kind of happened, I didn't even think about it, it was like, wow, this is easy. And it wasn't like I was thinking about those photos or anything, they just sort of got me in the mood. I don't know what I was thinking about, I really don't know. Maybe you."

"And?"

She sniffed and choked and said, "Yes." Her voice cracked on it, and she was crying and laughing again. "I did."

"It happened?"

"Yes. It was incredible. It really happened, just out of the blue and it was . . . just like all the books say. And, Jamie, I thought of you, because I know you said it would happen this way, that I would have to do it myself."

James was laughing deeply, pounding his fist on the glass. "And how was it?"

"It was unbelievable. It was marvellous." She laughed and cried and coughed. "And then I did it again, too. I feel all limp."

"I'm coming home right now."

"Okay."

He couldn't hang up.

She said, "Did you say something was wrong?"

"No no. Oh yes, I did, but it's not a big deal. I'm just going to be busy this week, and . . . it's kind of funny. I'll tell you all about it."

"Okay."

Another silence.

"Jamie?"

"Yes."

"I can't wait to see you."

He stepped into the air, blushing. It had started to snow. He walked along Queen, back towards the mall and the subway. He was moving fast, but he stopped in front of the skating rink because the guy in the Team Canada jersey was circling the rink alone in the bright light, one hand behind his back. The crowd had cleared the rink for him; they were all along the sides, watching. The jersey flashed red and white, an old jersey, a logo from the seventies, but familiar, the maple leaf slanted and cut in half. It touched James in some way he could not pinpoint, seeing it. The guy had built up a knifing speed, was whipping around the little rink doing crossovers the whole way, his body on a slant. It looked as if he was being swung at the end of a rope.

As he did his jump, a great spinning leap in the centre of the rink, the crowd oohed and applauded, and James saw it was the team logo from the first Canada Cup of 1976 and he laughed out loud without knowing why. The guy touched down like a gull on water and he bowed as he came to a stop at one end of the rink, sending up a shower of ice.

James shivered. The snow glittered in the fluorescence. The skaters were again filling the ice with pom-poms, leading teetering kids around, falling over. The white-and-red jersey was flickering out of sight behind the rink. He wanted to catch up with the guy, find out where to get one. And his throat was choked, which was silly. His eyes were watering because of the wind. He turned towards the subway entrance and moved quickly. It was just that he had actually watched that series as a kid, the great 1976 series with Tretiak and Kharlamov and Sittler and Lafleur, and he hadn't seen that jersey in years. There were now tears on his cheeks, which amazed him. It was silly, but it was just, perhaps, it must be just because he hadn't seen one in so long.

Outside the subway, the snow came down like light.

YOUNG WOMEN

Sharing

■

It is raining. Gregory sits at the kitchen table, reading the newspaper. From the living room, Janie is watching him. She sits on the futon couch ("Two in one!" Gregory is fond of shouting. "An uncomfortable bed by night, an even more uncomfortable sofa by day!"), her legs in thick tights that may be for running or dancing folded under her. She wears heavy grey socks and a sweatshirt; her ponytail is coming loose. She stares right at him through the kitchen door, at his unshaven face, his cropped hair, his concentration. His leg is bobbing rhythmically under the table. She calls, "Have you thought about Easter yet? My mother wants to know."

Gregory doesn't answer.

She waits for a second, pulling on strands of her ponytail, then says, "If we're supposed to be at your parents on Friday then we'll have to have some way of getting back into town Sunday."

She watches his foot waggling.

"Hello?"

He looks up. "What?"

"You do realize it's next weekend, this weekend?"

"Oh," says Gregory. "Yeah." He looks back down at the newspaper.

Janie sighs. She looks at the rainy window.

"Sakic's plus minus is plus *forty*," says Gregory, in the kitchen. "Can you believe that?"

"I guess," says Janie, "you don't want to talk about this."

"Not particularly. Unless you have something better for me, as a reward, like say having the underside of my tongue slit with razor blades."

"What?" says Janie.

Gregory is silent.

"It's the weekend," she says. "That's three days."

She watches his mouth moving slightly as he reads the scores.

"Look," she says, "I don't know what you're so pissed off about."

Gregory looks up. His face is distant. "What did you say?"

"Are you still pissed off about that . . . Never mind."

"I'm not pissed off about anything. I'm just trying to read the paper."

Janie looks out the window.

Leading from the living room is a narrow corridor hung with coats. There are several doors, leading to bedrooms furnished with milk crates filled with books and cherished vinyl records which are unplayable because no one has a turntable any more. The last door is closed. Behind it is a bedroom painted dark green. The bedroom is dim because the paper blind is down. It is warm and stuffy in the bedroom; Andrew's clothes litter the bed and floor. Andrew has Ellen up against a dresser. He has his arms around her waist and she has her arms around his neck. He is singing, barely beneath his breath, "Ahm, ahm, ahm jes a *luhv* machine, an ah doan *wuk* fuh nobody butchoo, baby. . ." He is wiggling his hips against hers, swinging his pelvis. He kisses her neck.

Ellen is trying not to laugh too loudly. She says, "How do I know your intentions are honourable?"

"My intentions," murmurs Andrew, his hands wandering, "are merely to help you clean up your outfit. Bit of dust on your collar here. Ash on your bustline, here, excuse me, just have to clean that up a little."

Ellen draws breath sharply, then says, "Mmmm."

"And one spot, here, under your ear . . ."

"Stop." She pushes him away. "We should get ready. We're supposed to be going to the art gallery with them."

"We've got time. Time to get on the *luuuuhhv train!*" His voice becomes a falsetto wail. "It's the *sooooul train!*"

"What happened to care about others? I thought that was your new motto. Care and compassion for others." She has her fingers twined in his hair.

"You should just *feel* the compassion I have for you, boy, I am just *swollen* with compassion."

"Do you care at all about others? Do you? Well, do you?"

"Well do ya, punk?" growls Andrew.

"Sssh. They're just in the living room. They can hear us."

"They'll be fine. They're having a fight. Nothing they love better. It makes them happy. Excuse me, I seem to have misplaced my hand. And there seems to be all this compassion in my *pants*, or something — "

"What, the love machine?"

"I am one." He sings, "*Roller coaster, slow down, doo DOOA doo doo. . .*"

In the living room, Janie hears his muffled singing. Her eyes dart to the bedroom door, closed, then back to Gregory's bowed head. He is still reading. She takes a deep breath and says, "Listen, we have to plan this, we can't —"

"That's exactly," says Gregory with unexpected sharpness, "what I don't understand." He still will not look up. "I don't understand why we can't."

"Wing it," says Janie. "I know. Wing it means I make all the decisions and I arrange everything."

"Fine with me. Listen. I'm a boy. Okay? I have a genetic disposition here. You want me to plan a menu too, like, what, make a casserole, bring it in a tupperware container, or what? I don't do that. I'm a boy."

Janie is silenced.

Gregory waits a moment, then bursts, "Okay. You know what the problem is? You know what my problem is? If it were up to me there would be no Easter, there would be no parents, there would be no buses and borrowing cars, and there would be no, I don't know, discussion of which of Granny's old china we want to take back with us, because it bores me, okay? It bores me stiff."

"So what do you suggest? You don't want to go? You want to stay here and watch hockey?"

"That is certainly what I want to do."

"Okay. Is that what we're going to do? We're going to call them and tell them we're not coming?"

He exhales loudly. He grits his teeth. "No. Of course we have to go."

"Okay. So we're no further ahead. We still have to decide how —"

"We have to waste a perfectly good, free, grown-up day talking about it, when we could be putting it off and having more of our lives to live." Gregory jerks his head towards the window. The rain is solid. It hides the world of bars and art galleries and intriguing laboratories and heroic football fields from them; it distorts the outside. It streaks the windows in bars. "Sometimes I think you want me to . . ." He trails off.

"I want you to what?"

"I don't know. Forget it." He looks back down at the newspaper.

"No, what? What?"

"I don't know. Write Christmas cards. Understand gardening. Be someone else."

This time Janie is silenced for a long moment. There is no sound but the muttering and giggling down the hall. Janie closes her eyes against it. She even puts her hands over her ears. But she removes them, in case Gregory says something she might not hear.

Finally, he says, "He's fifth in the league in points, too. I can't believe that."

Janie swings her legs to the floor. She stretches and says, "So are you ready to go?"

"And mister goddam great one Fedorov is just dropping off the map, like he's totally invisible."

"Are we going to the art gallery or not?"

Gregory folds the newspaper with resignation. "What makes you think," he says slowly, "that we're not?"

"Well, I thought we were going now."

Gregory pauses. He rubs his chin. A little less defiantly, he says, "Could we go later? Like late afternoon?"

"Well . . ." says Janie. Her voice rises in pitch. "It's just that . . . it's almost late afternoon now. I know you. If we don't make a move now then the whole day is just going to drift away and we'll never —"

"Well," says Gregory, "it doesn't sound as if Ellen and Andrew are exactly ready."

There is a muffled sound from the bedroom, a high girl's voice. It is a shriek or a gasp. Gregory pretends not to hear it. Janie jerks her eyes away from the corridor as if burned. She moves away from it, quickly, with agitation, towards the window. She looks outside.

In the bedroom, Andrew has succeeded in unbuttoning most of Ellen's shirt. He is kissing her naked shoulders and chest, nibbling at her bra straps and singing.

She says, "Ssh. I feel bad for them."

"For them?" he mutters. "They couldn't be happier. They can go on like that for hours. Days. Months."

"No, I mean it's mean to —"

"It's mean to be happy when they're not? Is that what you mean?"

"Well, to let them hear it, yes."

"Hear what?" He puts his hands on her breasts.

"Oh."

"That?"

"*Art gallery*," says Ellen.

"Schmallery. I love you. You have beautiful breasts. I'm going to call you Breasts from now on. Hey, beautiful Breasts. Or just

Jugs. Hey, Jugs. You like Jugs?"

"I feel so bad for them. It's just like they're trapped in here. And there's this big black cloud in whatever room they're in and I feel bad walking into it, like I have to be sad too, when I'm in it, you know? I don't know what her problem is. She just won't leave it alone, she has to keep at him to change, it's so sad. He's not going to change, she should just —"

"Would you shut up?" His fingertips are struggling with the hook of the bra between her shoulder blades. "Do you like it or not?"

"What?"

"I think it's pretty."

"What?"

"Jugs. Come here, Jugs."

"You are an asshole."

"Let's lie down for a second. I'm sleepy."

"No. Art gallery. Must reach art gallery."

He is pulling her towards the bed. "I can't go to the art gallery. I find it too eroticizing. All that Group of Seven. I'll explode. Rest. Must rest. You know most modern people don't get enough sleep. It's when you're in REM sleep that you get the most —"

They fall together on the bed. She stops him, half sits up. "Andrew. Can I ask you something?"

He is busy with her belt buckle, breathing hard. "I'm busy. You can leave a message with my secretary, and —"

"Was she like that when you went out with her?"

Just for a second, just for a very brief second, Andrew stops. Then he rolls on top of her, pinning her hands to the bed. He says, "Would you just stop talking please?"

In the living room, Janie hears her muffled giggle, and then a distinct whimper or moan. Gregory looks up for a second. He does not look at Janie. He frowns as he returns his gaze to the paper. Janie is watching him. She turns back to the window, a moving sheet of water. Her eyes are full of tears.

Chez
Giovanni

Margaret was punching numbers into the VISA terminal when Ellen stopped behind her. "Guess who's in your section."

Margaret looked around. "Mark? Because if it's Mark I can't fucking handle it, seriously, Ellen, you'll have to —"

"No, no, fuck, it's not Mark. It's someone famous."

Margaret peered over the bar, across the crowded tables. A big man in a black silk shirt had just sat with a young woman. He had a huge grey head and a slack jaw. "Is that —?"

"Skolnick. He's in town shooting the latest film. So lucky you. Be nice to him, maybe he's casting the next one, who knows?"

Margaret looked at the director's date, who appeared to be even taller than him. She had long red hair. "That's —"

"Anna Valgot. They always come in here. I think they're together."

"That's the chick he uses, right, she gets the lead in everything?"

Ellen nodded, narrowing her eyes as she looked at the woman. "She gets everything. She gets all the parts."

Margaret watched Anna Valgot as she crossed her fine ankles, her suede boots. Her hair was thick, her complexion glowing. She was about Margaret's age. She wore a black dress of indefinable material, a loose jacket of something crinkly; even Margaret could not guess where she had bought it. She watched as Anna Valgot tore a tiny piece from her roll, brought it almost to her lips, then placed it back on the plate, left it sitting neatly.

"Anna Valgot," said Margaret. "No way that's her real name. What kind of a name is that?"

"She's been reading too many Russian novels," said Ellen.

"Romances, more like it. I wonder what her real name is. She looks like a Rosedale girl. It's probably something Rosedale Wasp, like Jennifer. Jennifer McClellan. Jennifer Pearson."

Ellen snorted. "Robertson. Janet Robertson. There was a Janet Robertson at my high school. She sells real estate now. All RIGHT, I'm COMING," she shouted at the kitchen.

Margaret approached Skolnick's table with her pad. Skolnick was hunched over the table, his hands tense on the menu. He had eyebrows like steel wool.

"Ready to order?"

The red-haired girlfriend smiled at her. "I'll have the penne with clam sauce."

"Penne. Sir?"

Skolnick looked up and across the table at the woman. He looked dazed. "Penne," he said blankly.

"Pasta," said his girlfriend. "It's like thick spaghetti."

"Pasta," he said. "Okay. I like that. We'll have penne. And . . ." He frowned, holding the menu closer to his face.

A moment passed. Margaret shifted her weight from foot to foot, watching the tables fill up. "If you need a few more minutes, I can —"

"Scallops," said the filmmaker. "Have I had that?"

His girlfriend said, "They're the round seafood things. They're mushy and white. You like them."

"I do? I like them?"

"Yes," said the girlfriend. "Order them."

"Okay," he said, sighing. "I'll have the scallops."

"Okay," said Margaret. "One scallops, one penne, anything to start?"

"Hey!" said the filmmaker. He was pointing at the menu. "Zucchini." He looked up at Anna Valgot with wide eyes. "Zucchini. What is that, again?"

"It's the long green vegetable. You've had it."

"I've had it?"

"It's like cucumber," said Margaret.

"You like it," said the girlfriend.

"Zucchini?" He turned to look at Margaret. He appeared to be looking through her, far beyond her and the zucchinis. "We'll have zucchini to start."

"Well," said Margaret, "it's actually not a separate dish, it's part of the sauce on the penne, so you're getting some anyway, but if you like I can ask the kitchen to —"

"We've got zucchinis? We've got the zucchinis in there?"

"Yes."

"Okay." He sighed with relief. "We've got the zucchinis." He waved his hand vaguely and looked at Anna Valgot. "Okay?" She nodded. He handed the menus to Margaret with a wide smile. "Thank you."

As Margaret pushed through the kitchen doors she heard the shouting. Ellen was screaming, "Stop it! Stop it!", standing between Tikiri and Mohammed, Mohammed trying to reach around her to jab at Tikiri with something in his hand.

"Don't you ever!" Mohammed was screaming. "Don't you ever!"

The two dishwashers were standing around silently, arms folded. Unfinished plates were standing on the counter; a thick plume of smoke was rising from something on the grill.

Tikiri was muttering in Tamil, his jaw clenched, his fists bunched at his waist, glowering at Mohammed with flashing white eyes. "Go back to throwing rocks," he said. "You go back to the territories, you throw rocks at the jeeps all your life, go on, fuck you."

"STOP IT!" screamed Ellen, waving her arms between them.

"Ellen!" shouted Margaret. "What the —"

"They're going to kill each other," wailed Ellen.

Mohammed lunged around her, and Margaret saw the flash in his hand. Ellen shrieked; the dishwashers leapt back. Tikiri dodged the blade and grabbed Mohammed's arm. He pushed it onto a burner and Mohammed screamed, dropping the knife. The dishwashers darted in and separated them as Mohammed fell to the floor, clutching his hand.

"Call Giovanni," said Ellen, grabbing a towel. She leaned over Mohammed and wrapped his hand. He was shivering, his face contorted. Margaret looked over at Tikiri. He was leaning against the counter, panting.

He looked at her with wide eyes and turned both palms up. "He try to kill me," he said throatily.

"Jesus Christ," said Margaret, "what is that on the burner? Manoj, quick, get it off, Manoj. For Christ's sake. The smoke alarm will go off in a second. Ashot, get on a chair and disconnect the alarm, we'll have the fire department here again."

Mohammed stood up shakily, cradling his wrapped hand. He wasn't looking at Tikiri.

"Now," said Ellen, "are you guys finished or do we have to call Giovanni?"

"No call Giovanni," said Mohammed.

"All right," said Margaret. "If you guys are through trying to kill each other." She looked at Tikiri. He wiped his forehead with his sleeve and turned back to the stove. He began to scrape the burned lamb chops off the grill, cursing. She glanced through the windows in the swinging doors. "Giovanni is going to freak if he hears this. You do realize we are full out there, don't you? We are packed." She looked at Ellen. "What the hell was it about?"

"No clue. Someone got an order backwards."

Tikiri whirled around, his teeth bared. "I don't get no order backward," he yelled, pointing a spatula at Ellen's throat. "He fucking screw everything up —"

"All right," said Ellen.

"You bitch bastard face," said Mohammed from behind Margaret, in a wavering voice. "You fucking crazy man, you —"

"All RIGHT," shouted Margaret.

"Get him out of my kitchen," roared Tikiri. "Get him out or I will not work. I will not work with him."

"Call Giovanni," said Ellen.

Margaret slammed through the swinging doors; she was lunging at the phone beside the reservation book when it rang. She hesitated for a second, cursing. It rang again. She picked it up. "Good evening, Giovanni's?"

"Good evening," said a plummy voice. "How are you this evening?"

"How am I? A little busy," she said evenly. There were muffled shouts from the kitchen. "How can I help you?"

"I was kind of hoping for a reservation."

She turned to the book. "Yes sir. For when?"

"How about . . . Hmmm."

She counted seconds. The shouting in the kitchen seemed to have stopped again. "For tonight, sir? I'm afraid we're all booked up tonight."

"No, no." He giggled. "No no *no*, not for to*night*. For heaven's sake." He found this very amusing. "For *Tues*day."

"Tuesday. Fine. What time?"

"Oh, say . . ."

She could hear him breathing. "Sir, I'm a little busy right now. Could you call back in a little while? Thank you." She squelched him with a fingertip.

She held the button down, counted to five, then punched Giovanni's home number, which was pinned to the wall in warning red ink.

It rang and rang, and then she got his machine with its friendly musical message. She waited for the interminable gypsy guitar to end. "Hi Giovanni, it's Margaret at the restaurant, listen, are you there? Hello? Because if you are you should pick up the phone. Hello?"

She looked around the room. People were staring at her, looking at watches ostentatiously, tapping fingertips on tablecloths. Then she noticed the film director: Skolnick had laid his head on the table. Anna Valgot was clutching his hand, talking to him intensely.

"Okay," said Margaret into the phone, "you're not home. Listen, I know you really don't want to hear this but I think you should get down here. There's a bit of a problem. Bye."

As soon as she hung up the phone rang again. She ignored it. Ellen emerged from the kitchen with two plates of food. "It's okay," she said. "Mohammed is sitting out back alone. He won't go to a hospital, and he won't have a drink, but I think he's calming down. We've taken Ashot off the dishes and he's doing salads and prep."

"Ashot?"

"Tikiri's training him as he goes."

"*Ashot?*"

"I'm sure it'll be fine. Just we're a little bit behind now, and things are going to slow down a little."

"I'll hand out a few free drinks." Margaret heard a low drone from the front; it sounded like a moan. She looked back at Skolnick. He was rolling his head over the table and muttering loudly. A couple at a neighbouring table were craning their necks to watch. Anna Valgot was still clutching his hand, but now looking around her, smiling tightly.

"She's having a hard time," said Margaret.

"Well," said Ellen, "she's dealing with it *perfectly*, isn't she? As I'm sure she deals with everything. She is perfect."

Margaret puffed out her cheeks. "Fucking Jesus Christ."

"Marg, your food will be up in a second. You call Giovanni?"

"He's not home."

"Marg, we're going to need him."

"I know."

"It's just that if Mohammed decides to come back in —"

"El, I *know*. Oh, *shit*."

Four suits stood in the entrance, shaking umbrellas, ties loose, shoving each other. The worst kind.

"I'll do them," said Ellen. "Your food is up." She grabbed four menus. Margaret watched her tight haunches in the black miniskirt swing through the tables. She could imagine the smile Ellen was giving them. She saw the suits' red faces light up as Ellen approached them, their jaws opening wetly. Margaret turned and went back into the kitchen.

She approached Skolnick's table with the two dishes. "Penne with clam sauce, and . . . scallops."

"Thank you," said the girlfriend brightly. She was still squeezing his hand. Skolnick was wagging his head, his mouth open. He looked up at Margaret as if startled. His eyes were unfocused. Suddenly he spread both arms wide, hitting her in the groin. Margaret jumped back.

"Barry," said Anna Valgot sharply.

"Limitless!" said Skolnick loudly. "Vast void!" He seemed on the verge of tears.

"*Barry!*"

Margaret set the dishes down and was about to turn when she saw something flash in the window behind Skolnick's head, the one that gave onto the alleyway. She looked up and saw Mark's face, white in the darkness outside. He was staring at her grimly, his face hanging over the mad Skolnick like a moon.

Margaret clamped her jaws together with a click. She spun

around and made for the kitchen. Diners waved at her, they said, "Excuse me, *excuse* me!", they clicked their fingers as she passed. She stared straight ahead. The tableful of suits, already fixed with rum and Cokes and light beers — thank God for Ellen, she thought, she's so fast — smiled aggressively at her. "Hi," said one, nodding, his eyes slightly crossed. She ignored him.

The kitchen was quiet. Tikiri started and pirouetted as she entered, raising a cleaver. Ashot was carefully patterning a plate with red and yellow pepper coulis, his forehead knotted, a pink triangle of tongue protruding from his pursed mouth.

"For God's sake, Tikki."

"You." He put the cleaver down, turned back to the grill. "Make sure he does not come in here."

"Not too much, Ashot," said Margaret.

Ashot looked up at her, his face in wild distress.

"That's good though. You're doing great."

Manoj, now alone at the dishes, turned his head to scowl at her. There was a thumping at the back door, a muffled yell.

"Is that —"

"I lock him out," said Tikiri majestically.

"You've *locked* — Tikiri, there's no gate onto that courtyard. He's trapped out there."

Mohammed's rain-streaked face appeared at the back window, and his fist. He pounded and screamed.

"Not coming in," said Tikiri, his back turned. "Ashot, bring plate for sauce."

"Tikki, it's raining out there."

Tikiri turned and raised the cleaver again, and Mohammed's face disappeared.

Ellen whirled in. "Marg, three and seven are getting pretty upset, you might want to get some drinks to them."

"Okay. Tikki, three is —"

"Three is carpaccio and polenta with funghi," he shouted. "I know. Seven is quail and seafood special, of course I know, it's written right here, you think I am blind? I can't read?"

Margaret put a hand to her forehead. "Yes, Tikki, I know you know."

He was waving his arms around again now. "How you expect me hurry with no sous-chef, Ashot, Ashot —"

"Shut up Tikiri," said Margaret. "Shut the fuck up. Ellen. Listen. Mark is here."

Ellen stopped, her arms laden with salads. "What?"

"He's outside. He's just hanging around in the alleyway, peering in at us."

Ellen stared at the ceiling, a salad at the end of each outstretched arm. Finally, she said, "Marg, I can't deal with that right now. I'm sorry. I just can't." And she was through the doors.

Margaret leaned against the prep counter for a few seconds. The phone was still ringing. She straightened and went to the bar to pour free glasses of house white.

She gave some out and removed four plates and took four more orders and approached the most recent arrivals, a two. A dark-haired man in his thirties, jacket and tie, and a bright blonde in a tight dress.

"Let us talk about wine," said the man. A French accent. He pointed at the wine list. "Where are the Bordeaux?"

Margaret drew a breath. "Under France."

"Mmmhh," said the man.

"He likes Bordeaux," said the young woman eagerly, "He's

French." She must have been about twenty-two. She had the accent of the suburbs. Margaret had a sudden unbidden vision of a discount bulk pet food store in a strip mall. She shook her head slightly. "He's from France," said the girl. "He's European."

The man looked up at Margaret triumphantly. "Not many Bordeaux."

Instead of saying, "*This being an Italian restaurant, no,*" she said, "We have some Barolos that you might like, down here." And she couldn't resist adding, "Under Italy."

"Hmmm." The man frowned, stroked his chin.

"Take your time," said Margaret, and fled before he responded.

She was at the bar when Mark came in.

He didn't wait to be seated. He threw one long leg after the other until he was at the recently abandoned four right next to the director and his girlfriend. It was still covered with dishes and ashtrays. He pushed the plates away from him with a clatter, knocking over a glass, and sat heavily.

Margaret turned away. At the VISA terminal, her back still to him, she considered. The table was in her section, but she could get Ellen to serve him. As long as Giovanni didn't arrive right now. Giovanni would blame her for having him in the restaurant.

She glanced quickly at Mark. He had sprawled his legs into the only free passage between the tables, and he had lit a cigarette, in the non-smoking section. He wore his leather jacket and had tucked his camouflage pants into his knee-high Docs. His hair was long and stringy and wet, and he jerked his head around querulously, like a chicken, which told Margaret that he was drunk. He looked right at her and contorted his lower face into something possibly meant to be a smile.

Margaret turned away again. She waited for Ellen to pass. "El —"

"I know. I've seen him. Marg, honestly, I can't deal with him right now."

"El, *please*."

Ellen exhaled. "Jesus Christ." She peered around the cash at Mark. "He probably just wants to see you."

"Yes. Yes he does just want to see me."

"He looks calm. We can't just throw him out for nothing."

"Throw him out? We can't throw him out even if we wanted to. The best thing is just to keep him calm."

"Marg, you're going to have to talk to him at some point."

Margaret felt her stomach contract, and tears gathering somewhere, as if in her throat or at the back of her head.

She took two more orders and approached Mark. She tried to smile. "Hi."

He said, "Hi." He tried to smile too. Apparently he had been trying to grow a goatee. "How are you?"

"Really, really busy. You want to see a menu?"

Mark's upper lip curled. "Menu. No I don't want to see a menu."

"You want a drink?"

"I wanted to talk to you. About us."

Margaret lifted her face to the ceiling, then back down. "Listen, this is really the wrong place, I've told you a thousand times before, I'm *way* too busy —"

"Here we go again."

"And besides, there is absolutely nothing to talk about. I don't know what to tell you, Mark. I really don't." Margaret was aware that she was standing close enough to Anna Valgot for her to hear everything. She glanced to one side and saw that the filmmaker was quiet again, eating steadily, his face close to the plate. He was snuffling and muttering as he ate. The woman was staring right at her. Her face was expressionless.

Margaret turned back to Mark, feeling her own face heating up. More quietly, she said, "Mark, this is really not the time. Please please please don't give me a hard time tonight. I think you should leave."

"Just like that, eh? Heard that before. That's your answer to everything, isn't it?"

Margaret looked around in embarrassment. Skolnick was still eating, but letting out an occasional whimper. Anna Valgot was still watching her closely. This time Margaret caught her eye, and Anna Valgot canted her head and gave a little half smile. There was something questioning about it, something sympathetic, something even a little sad.

"The band is doing really good," said Mark.

"That's good."

"We're playing Sneaky Dee's in a benefit."

"That's great," said Margaret seriously. "That's terrific. Who for?"

"Who for? Oh." Mark frowned. "Helping House. I think."

"Helping House? What's that?"

"Oh. What is it?" Mark frowned harder, bit his lip. He squinted up at the ceiling to concentrate. Finally he said, "Tards, I think."

"What?"

"I think it's tards, this one. It's like this home for learning disabilities or autistics or quads or something, you know, retards. Something like that. I forget."

"Oh." Margaret glanced around again. "Well, anyway, that's —"

"Oh, and bicycle lanes."

"Oh. Good. Well, that's terrific for you. Can I get you anything?"

"I don't know why we had to break up," he said, his voice quavering.

Slowly she said, "Oh. My. God." She took a deep breath, pulled out her pad. "So do you want anything?"

"You still have some of my *stuff*," said Mark in a high voice, his eyes darting.

"Your stuff?" Margaret opened her eyes wide. She couldn't leave it alone; she said, "What stuff? I do not have any of your stuff. I put everything, *everything* in Todd's van when he came. I even put some of *my* stuff in."

Mark was shaking his head. "I can't find a place that nice," he whined, "ever again. It'll never be nice like that. I don't understand."

"Listen, I should tell you that Giovanni is going to be here any minute."

Mark curled his lips again. "So what? So what are you trying to say? He's going to beat me up? He's going to call the cops on me?" He was speaking too loudly. Margaret stared at the tablecloth. "You can't kick me out for no good reason," Mark almost shouted. "I have a right to sit here just like anybody else."

"Yes," said Margaret as quietly as she could. "As long as you order something."

Mark looked across his table and noticed Anna Valgot. Margaret looked too: the actress was staring straight at Mark, her eyes unwavering, her mouth set. It was sheer ice.

Mark looked away. "I'll have an Ex."

"One Export," said Margaret. "Fine. Coming up." She whirled away.

She reemerged from the kitchen just in time to see Giovanni's Alfa pull up outside, shining black in the rain. She ducked back into the kitchen to warn them. And to give him time to see Mark.

She had a plate in one hand and Mark's bottle of beer in the other and was about to exit when the doors swung open and Giovanni erupted in a gust of cologne. Ellen was behind him, talking fast. He wore his soft sheepskin jacket, a silk shirt. His sleek eyebrow quivered as he saw Margaret. "Margaret," he said with distaste. "I've been calling, nobody's answered the phone. What's going on?"

"— and he's outside now," said Ellen, "we've locked him in the courtyard, and he's calm, I think, he's smoking, but you should talk to him."

"You've *locked* him in the *courtyard?*" said Giovanni.

The window rattled as Mohammed rapped on it again. His face hovered in the darkness outside, blurry with rain. His eyes reminded Margaret forcefully of a documentary she had just seen on the suicide squads of Hezbollah. She said simply, "Yikes."

"All right," said Giovanni. "Everybody out of the kitchen except Tikiri. Ashot, get us a bottle of cognac and three glasses, and leave us alone. Everybody out."

As Margaret edged past him with her plate, he grabbed her arm. "Hey," he said, leaning close to her. She could see the flecks of grey in his moustache, smell the leather of his coat. "I don't want him here while you're working. I've told you."

"Who?" said Margaret, trying to smile.

"You know who. Your boyfriend."

"Giovanni, I told you, he's not my boyfriend. I didn't ask him here, Giovanni, in fact —"

"I want him to leave, all right?" His voice was deep and calm.

"Giovanni, I — how can I —"

"Just ask him to leave, would you? Now quick, leave us alone here, quick quick." His hand in the small of her back, he pushed her through the swinging doors.

She delivered the food and then the beer without giving Mark time to speak. The Frenchman ordered a cheap Chianti. She removed the plates from the filmmaker's table, and he immediately put his head back down on the cloth and began making eerie high-pitched noises. Margaret hesitated before moving away. "Is he going to be all right?"

Anna Valgot bunched her lips. "I'm not sure, to tell you the truth. He's having a crisis. He gets like this."

For the first time, Margaret noticed something in her voice, an accent. It reminded her of the French exchange program she had done when she was fourteen, at Chicoutimi.

"NOTHING!" Skolnick shouted suddenly, into the tablecloth. "Nothing at all, just a VOID, and it's INFINITE!"

Anna Valgot shook her long hair. It glowed orange in the candlelight. She grasped Skolnick's hand again, extended on the tablecloth, and he quietened instantly. She studied his big, dark lolling head for a second, nervously, but he was still, muttering quietly to himself. "Listen," she said, "I'm sorry about this, but it may be a problem getting him out of here. He has these — these moments and then he can get kind of agitated." There was a hoarseness to her voice, too, the kind you expect of heavy smokers. And the accent was definitely French, Canadian French.

"What are you saying?"

"Well, if I could call his — there's one guy who is good with him in these situations. His analyst. He has this personal analyst who comes and gets him and they talk and they go through this visualization process and all that, I don't know." Anna Valgot, made a gesture with her hand, as if to reach for her purse, but stopped. "I wish I had a cigarette." She dropped the h on "had."

"You're in the non-smoking section," said Margaret.

"No, no, I know. I don't smoke anyway."

"Excuse me!" someone called from across the room.

"Well, listen," said Margaret, "whatever, you can use the phone over there if you like, but — look, I just can't help you right now. We're having a kind of a stressful night in the kitchen and —-"

"And him," said the actress, nodding at Mark. Her mouth had turned down at the edges.

"Yeah." Margaret felt herself blushing. "That's a long story. But the owner's here now and, and he's in the kitchen now, and . . ."

"Ex*cuse* ME!"

Margaret felt herself trailing off, her legs trembling. She felt tears coming, a huge need to sit down. She steadied herself with the table edge.

Lightly, Anna Valgot touched her hand. "What's going on?"

Margaret rubbed her face, avoiding looking at Mark. "The chefs are fighting. The head chef here, he's a Tiger."

The actress smiled. "What do you mean, a tiger?"

"No, a Tiger. A Tamil Tiger. He was, anyway, before he came here. He's a refugee. He was a guerilla fighter."

"Oh." Anna Valgot nodded, as if unsurprised.

"And the sous-chef — anyway, never mind. I've got to go."

"What about him?" said Anna Valgot, nodding at Mark.

"Oh, him." Margaret disengaged her hand. "It's a long story."

"No, I mean, you need any help, you let me know." Her voice was surprisingly hard, with that cigarette edge and echo of Montreal. Outremont, Margaret thought, and shopping on St. Denis; she could see the dark glasses and copies of *Le Monde* in the Café Cherrier, and all the other immaculate women who looked like Anna Valgot.

"Thanks." She moved away.

She took some more orders but hesitated at the kitchen doors. No one had come in or out for fifteen minutes. Ellen approached, and stopped there, too. There was an odour of cigar smoke.

Ellen put her ear to the door. "They're laughing," she said. "They're fucking laughing in there." She leaped back as Giovanni pushed open the doors. He had a smile and a lit cigar.

"All right," he said. "Everything's okay."

Margaret peered around him and saw Mohammed and Tikiri sitting on the prep counter, smoking cigars and laughing. They had both taken their aprons off.

"Jesus Christ," said Margaret.

"Give them a few minutes," said Giovanni, "before you put any more orders."

"Holy shit, Giovanni," said Ellen. "You are incredible."

"What did you do?" said Margaret. "How the hell did you know what to say to them?"

Giovanni smiled wearily. He put the bottle of cognac back on the shelf and crooked a finger at the two waitresses. "Look here."

He pointed to the map that was tacked to the wall behind the bar, the map that was invisible from the front. It was a street map of a city, with names marked in Italian. "This is Catania." Ellen and Margaret moved close to the map, breathing in the cigar smoke and staring, too tired to know what they were looking at.

Giovanni said, "Catania is a town in Sicily, a large town. A very old town. A port. Very dangerous. This here —" He put his finger on a tight web of streets in the northeast corner, tiny streets. "This is a neighbourhood called Reggio, or, we called it, Il Cavolo." He paused for a second, smiling grimly. "And this street here, this curvy one" — he traced it carefully — "is called the Via Vecchia."

He withdrew his finger and turned to the women. "And that is the street where I grew up." He took a long pull on his cigar.

The gypsy guitar CD had ended, and the restaurant was suddenly silent. Margaret looked around the room, now emptying out. The suits were still drinking, but their heads were leaning to the centre of the table, each telling a breathless story in turn. Mark had finished his beer and was drumming absorbedly on the table-top with both palms. Skolnick was quiet, his head in his hands. Anna Valgot was talking to him again, very softly.

"Who is that guy?" said Giovanni calmly.

"Barry Skolnick," said Ellen. "He's a famous filmmaker. He made *Milwaukee, U.S.A.*"

"And *Rock Highway*."

Giovanni raised his eyebrows. "*Rock Highway?* I have heard of it. Barry Skolnick. Well well. And the girl?"

"Woman," said Ellen automatically.

Margaret said quickly, "She's the lead — the star in all his movies."

"Yes," said Giovanni, nodding. "Well well. Good."

"He's crazy," said Margaret. "He's being a nuisance."

Giovanni frowned. "Make sure he gets good treatment. Eh?"

"If he doesn't scare everybody away."

Giovanni was buttoning his jacket. "You brought me away from a party," he said sadly. "Sophia called me there when she got your message. But I'm going home now. So you call me there if there's any more trouble. Eh?" He winked.

At the door he looked at Mark with open contempt. He called to Margaret, "You remember what I say, eh?" He turned, and stopped again. "And what's with the music? Put a new CD on."

As soon as he had left, Margaret approached Mark. "I think you should go now."

He looked up at her. He was even paler now, his jaw clenched. "I'll have another Ex, please."

Anna Valgot's voice came sharply across the table. "Don't give it to him." She was staring the death-ray stare at Mark.

Margaret hesitated. Mark looked stunned. He opened his mouth and closed it. In the candlelight, in her black jacket, Anna Valgot looked, Margaret had to admit, unbelievably beautiful.

"Listen, mister rock 'n roll," said Anna Valgot. "We're sick of the tough-guy shit, okay?"

"Tough guy?" said Mark uncertainly.

In the moment of hesitation, Margaret tried to move away, but he caught her wrist and held it.

"Mark," she said deliberately, "let go of my wrist."

Anna Valgot stood up. No one had put a new CD on. In a clear, hard voice she said, "Let go of her arm. Or I call the cops. Right now."

Mark turned red. He said, "Hey," and trailed off. Several heads were turned, watching him. He blinked several times, his eyes filling with tears.

He dropped her arm, pushed back his chair and stood up,

swaying. He said, "You fucking bitch," and pushed a wineglass off the table so it smashed.

Anna Valgot and Margaret stood still. He rubbed at his eyes frantically, then turned and staggered out the door. Margaret watched him lurch all the way down the street, and she let all the air out of her lungs in one long stream.

The tables began to clear more rapidly after that. The Frenchman and the bimbo cancelled their dessert order. Only the suits were still laughing violently, oblivious.

Anna Valgot got up gently, careful not to disturb the moaning Skolnick. Margaret, clearing dishes, pointed to the phone. After the actress had made her phone call, Margaret stopped her at the bar and touched her shoulder. "Thanks," she said.

"Oh." Anna Valgot shrugged. "Listen —"

Just then Skolnick exploded. "BLACK HOLE!" he shrieked, "IT'S ALL A BIG FUCKING BLACK HOLE!" He was sitting straight up, his twisted face towards the ceiling, his arms flailing wide.

Anna Valgot rushed to him and stood behind him. She put her arms around his neck and spoke intently into his ear.

But he was too upset. "And what happens *then?*" he whimpered. "What happens, what happens when we DIE DIE DIE!" There were tears on his cheeks. The suits had stood up to watch. "DIE DIE DIE!"

He tried to stand, but Anna Valgot forced him down.

Margaret was at her side. "Did you get the analyst?"

"I left a message," said Anna Valgot, struggling. "He's out."

"Listen," said Margaret, "let's get him downstairs."

One of the suits had approached unsteadily. "Need some help here, ladies?"

"No thank you," said Anna Valgot quickly. "Downstairs? What's downstairs?"

"A storeroom," said Margaret. "It's quiet. There's a chair in it, and a door we can lock."

"Is there a window?"

Margaret shook her head.

"Good. Okay. Until Donny comes."

"Donny?"

"The therapist. His system pages him automatically, in an emergency. He'll come."

"Donny!" wailed Skolnick, covering his face with his hands. "Donny! I can't do it! I can't shrink it like you told me, shrink, shrink shrink shrink."

"Come on, honey," said Anna Valgot softly into Skolnick's ear. "Sweetheart. Come with me. Baby. It's okay."

"Conquer," he said, breathing heavily. "Shrink it down. Kill it. DOMINATE."

He was still talking and shouting as she and Margaret stood him up, lifting gently by the armpits. Margaret had to keep brushing away the eager helpful arms of the young suit. They walked him slowly through the appalled diners to the back staircase, then, carefully, down the narrow stairs to the basement. He let himself be led, shaking his head. At the bottom, Margaret went ahead, clearing the cases of beer bottles and bags of garbage. She opened the storeroom door.

Anna Valgot took Skolnick in and sat him on the chair. He was quieter. "Thanks," she said. "And I'm sorry about all this. Just leave us here. And call me if Donny shows up. I'm Anna, by the way."

"I know," said Margaret.

An hour later the last table left. Tikiri and Mohammed left separately, saying nothing to the waitresses. Ashot and Manoj were still in the kitchen, washing. Margaret began her cash.

"Marg," said Ellen, lifting a chair onto a table, "are they still down there?"

Margaret looked at the door to the basement stairs. "I guess so."

"What the hell are they doing down there?"

Margaret looked out the big front windows. The rain had turned to sleet and the street was empty. "I wonder what's happened to this mythical mystical therapist. He was supposed to come and wave his wand and cure the guy."

"The magic analyst."

Margaret glanced as Ellen finished the chairs, swinging them up and slamming them down with a grace that Margaret had always admired, a practised precision. It was like watching a carpenter hammering.

"Well *Marg*, if he doesn't show up in the next five minutes we're going to have to turf them out anyway. Won't that be fun."

"I'll do it," said Margaret quickly. "You go home if you want." She tried counting the VISA bills again. "*Fuck*. Ninety-five, ninety-seven . . . *Fuck*. I don't get it."

Ellen took off her apron and lit a cigarette. She leaned against the bar and began rolling her head around, stretching her neck. "At least we know how she gets all the parts."

Distractedly, trying not to lose count, Margaret said, "I thought she was okay in *Rock Highway*."

Ellen snorted. "Okay? Her *tits* were okay. She's got great tits, I'll give her that. She can't *act* her way out of a beer commercial. And she was just *totally* miscast in that."

"I thought she was pretty natural."

"Listen," said Ellen, uncorking a bottle of house red, "*I* know how she can act. I worked with her once."

Margaret sighed deeply, dropping the stack of receipts. "Okay. Start over." She began to add again.

"On one of Tivo Korecky's dance-slide things," said Ellen, pouring wine. "When she was still artsy. You remember him, the multimedia guy, who disappeared? She thought Tivo was a genius, a total *genius*. Actually we all did. That's why we all took our clothes off in every show, because you didn't question genius and the guy couldn't just be a letch, right? And besides." She paused, taking a long drag. "Even if we all knew he was just a letch it was nice to have an excuse to take your clothes off in front of people, including people you knew, like your roommates would be there and everything. And they would be like really blasé afterwards and no one mentioned it because it was big A art, so it was kind of an excuse. I always want to anyway. Don't you?"

"Aha," said Margaret, riffling through the receipts. "I think I have it now. What?" She looked up. "Don't I what?"

Ellen swallowed the last of her wine and burped. "Don't you want to take off your clothes in front of your roommates?"

Margaret considered. "I don't think so. No. I don't have any roommates at the moment, anyway."

"Oh. I do. Anyway." Ellen turned back to the bar. "Let's see. What has lots in it? Australian white, God help us." She poured herself a second glass, inaccurately. "You want some? You just have to hold your nose."

Margaret scrutinized the bottle. "Not from that one, no, he'll notice it if it's gone down a lot. I'll have a Scotch."

Ellen recited in her waitress voice, "Laphroaig, Lagavulin, Dalwhinnie, Glenmorangie . . ."

"More left in the Lagavulin. No one ever orders it anyway, I don't know why he bothers."

"Excellent choice." Ellen reached for the shot glasses. "Anyway, she was pretty uptight about all that, but she didn't want to admit it to anyone, and you could tell she was really scared. She kept making excuses about how out of shape she was and then her clothes come off and it turns out she's like a skeleton. She's skinny as a rake. And I'm like ooops, body-problem city, *hel*-lo. Betty Bulimia, here we come."

Margaret was counting bills. "Well," she said quietly, "El, who didn't?"

Ellen took another drag. "Yeah. Well. Anyway, I guess she was okay in that. I don't remember. It was a stupid piece. She wasn't bad but she wasn't anything special. So I don't get why she's famous and now here we are."

Margaret entered the totals in the ledger. "I auditioned with her once. She wouldn't remember me. It was a beer commercial, funny enough. Neither of us got it. But we were at the same stage, then."

Manoj came out of the kitchen in his new Raptors jacket, drying his hands, nodding mutely.

"All done?" said Ellen.

Manoj nodded vigorously. "Finish. You want, you want I help . . . ?"

"No," said Margaret, "thanks, I'll make the deposit myself. That's okay. You go on home."

Ashot emerged a few minutes later, too tired even for his English lesson, which was a relief for Margaret, and he left in his new Blue Jays cap and his new Chicago Bulls jacket.

Ellen stubbed her cigarette. "Well," she said, looking at her watch. "Eddie's playing at the Horseshoe and the last set probably just ended, and I said I'd try to . . . You sure you don't want me to go down there with you?"

"Go," said Margaret. "I'll kick them out."

"Go *girl*. Are you sure? What if he goes berserk or something, starts throwing things or something?"

"I think they'll be okay. She handles him okay. He's been pretty quiet now, anyway. I haven't heard a peep."

Ellen had her leopard coat on and her black baseball cap. "Thanks, sweetie."

"Say hi to Eddie and them."

They hugged and kissed and Ellen left. Margaret locked the front door and turned off all the lights but the one over the bar.

She was moving towards the door to the basement when she saw Mark's face again, pressed against the glass of the same window, the window to the alleyway. She screamed. He stood outside in the sleet for a second, staring in at her, his white face the only visible part of him in the darkness. Then he turned and vanished.

Margaret turned off the bar light and sat in darkness for a moment, so that no one outside could see in. Then she went to all the windows and made sure they were tightly closed. She couldn't see Mark anywhere outside. Then she locked the side door and the door to the rear courtyard. She turned off the lights in the kitchen.

As she reemerged she heard a door opening and jumped.

"Are you okay?" came Anna Valgot's voice.

"Jesus Christ."

"Sorry. I'm right here by the basement door."

Margaret flicked the light on. "I was just going to come down and tell you. We're closed." She was trembling.

Anna came towards her. She had tied her hair back and her face looked narrow and white. "What's the matter? Was that you who screamed?"

"Yes. Sorry. I just got a fright. That guy, Mark, who left, he's back. I just saw him outside."

Anna looked around. "You lock all the doors?"

"Yes. Listen, how is . . ."

"Barry's asleep. He's fine. No sign of Donny, the analyst?"

Margaret shook her head. "Listen, if we wake him up — Barry, if we wake up Barry, is he going to freak out again?"

Anna frowned, and Margaret noted with interest the lines on her forehead, around her eyes. All her lipstick had come off. "I don't know, to tell you the truth. He could have forgotten all about it, or he could . . ." She trailed off. "Are those your cigarettes?"

"Sure. Here."

They both lit cigarettes. Margaret said, "Listen, thanks again for your help with . . . with that guy. You want some wine? Or some of this Scotch? It's excellent."

"You have rye?"

"Rye whisky?" Margaret frowned. "I think so. That's like Canadian Club, right?"

"Whatever. I like rye and ginger."

"Sure." Puzzled, Margaret found the bottles and glasses. She refilled her own glass. Anna was calling the psychiatrist again, leaving another message. Margaret rubbed her neck with both hands. As she relaxed, she felt the tears closer, pooling behind her eyes.

Anna pulled two chairs off a table. Margaret sat and loosened the laces on her drill boots. She pulled down another chair and put her stockinged feet on it.

Anna was drinking in rapid sips, smoking with quick puffs. "You're in the business too, right?"

Margaret was surprised. "Yes. I guess. I haven't worked for a while. How did you know?"

"I saw you in a show."

"You did?"

"It was at the Fringe or at Rhubarb, it had three women in it, I think, I think it was about a woman poet —"

"Sylvia Plath. Yes. You saw that?"

"And there was a painter in it too, she was Spanish or something."

Margaret giggled. "Frida Kahlo. It was a really stupid play. These famous women were supposed to meet in the afterlife." She sighed. "Oh. My. God."

"You were really good in that. I could never do difficult acting like that."

Margaret shrugged, pursed her lips.

"And we auditioned together once, too, for a beer commercial, but you probably don't remember. There were a lot of people there."

Margaret laughed outright. "That's funny. That's really funny. I do remember. I thought you wouldn't —" She flinched and stopped speaking, seeing a shape move outside.

"What?"

"Nothing. I thought I saw . . . He might be waiting for us to leave. Listen, do you mind if I turn the light off, so he can't see in? It gives me the creeps."

"Sure."

Margaret switched off the light. They sat in darkness with their feet up, in the smell of stale cigarettes and wine and the stubborn pall of garlic and fat. She drew a breath. "So. How did you get . . . how did you get involved with Barry?"

Anna shrugged. "The usual way. I auditioned for his first feature, *Eviscerated,* and I got the part. And then I slept with him. While we were shooting."

There was a silence. Margaret could hear the freezing rain tapping on the awnings. From outside came the occasional swish of passing taxis. The table was striped with a bar of orange light from the lamp in the alleyway. She thought of acting in a film and there was a coldness in her stomach, a pain. Her throat knotted. In a small voice, she said, "One break. One big break and that was it for you, hey?"

When Anna replied, her voice was small too. "It's not . . . it's not all great, you know. All this taking care of him."

Involuntarily, Margaret made a small hissing noise. "But you're famous." She felt the tears emerge now and drip on her face. "It must be rough. Must be really rough, taking care of a millionaire." She thought of Mark, his stringy hair, and her face crumpled up. "It's not like a fucking restaurant. Nothing is like this."

"I know all about that," said Anna. "I did it for ten years."

"Sure you did," Margaret sniffled. "Where? L'Express?"

"Saint John."

"The Saint John." Margaret wiped her eyes. "I don't know it. I don't remember it, anyway. Was that Damian Buhr's first restaurant?"

Anna laughed shortly. "No, it's a city. A town. In New Brunswick."

"Oops." Margaret gulped her whisky. Her tears wouldn't stop. "Sorry. Is that where you're from?"

"Sort of. I'm from the country, around there. I'm from a place called Buctouche, near Moncton. I went to Saint John to go to the big city. I worked in a truck stop, like a diner place."

"For *ten years?*"

"And in a bar. A few bars."

They smoked in silence.

"Wow," said Margaret. "Wow. So — do you mind me asking you this, I hope you don't think it's rude, but I always wanted to ask you, is that your real name?"

"My real name?" said Anna in surprise. "Of course it is. Sure it is. It's an Acadian name."

Margaret finished her whisky. She felt like laughing. Acadian. She took a long drag. She could feel the alcohol in her blood now, spreading along her limbs like moving sand. The wind rattled the windows, the ones that kept Mark out there, perhaps wandering alone in the rain.

She had a picture in her head of wind like this on a New Brunswick shoreline, a stone-grey sea, weedy grasses on a dune, mailboxes marked "LeBlanc." Wooden houses with satellite dishes, unpaved roads. A cinder-block pub called the King's Court. The Load of Mischief.

She tried to smile across the table at Anna Valgot. Her face was hidden.

"Listen," said Anna. "If you really want to work with Barry I can talk to him. He's about to cast, you know. That's why he's here."

The windows were gradually disappearing under ice. Outside, the city would be closed up in the storm, no one on the streets. The orange light glowed cold through the blurry windows. Margaret rubbed her face. Her fatigue was pressing down on her. It would be freezing on her way to the bank, on her way home.

She tried to think about auditioning for Skolnick and felt nothing but exhaustion. "I should," she said, and shivered. She got up and went to the coat rack to find her cardigan, and she kept thinking of Buctouche, New Brunswick: an auto-body shop with rusting pickups outside. A dog tied up next to a mobile home. She didn't know if it made her sad or happy.

Suddenly, she said, "No. Thanks. It's really not worth it. I really don't think I'm into it any more."

"What, the movie, or —"

"The whole business." She blew out her cheeks. "I've just decided."

"Okay." Anna paused, drinking. "You sure?"

"Yes. I'm sure."

"Okay. Whatever." She put her feet on the floor with a swish of crinkly skirt. "Well, listen, we should make your deposit. I'll come with you, and then we'll wake him and get him into a taxi. Okay?"

Margaret sat with her drink, feeling the tension ebbing from her body. She shivered as the windows rattled again. "It's turning into quite a storm." She looked around the dim restaurant, the neat rows of bottles behind the bar, the exposed beams of the ceiling, the hanging oriental rugs, grateful for the darkness. Her body was hollowing, something invisible emptying from it. Cigarette smoke hung in the orange ray. She couldn't see Anna's face, but she could hear her exhaling the smoke, the clink of the ice in her glass.

She could see the shoreline, a sluggish ferry, the scrubby little trees blasted by sea wind. And a wooden church with a stone Virgin outside, and lobster traps, and Acadian flags ripped up by the wind. Her tears had stopped completely now. She could see it clearly. "Let's just finish this drink. Let's just stay here for a while."

Dreams

Ellen has a secret but she doesn't know it. Only Eddie knows her secret. He lies awake at night listening to her talk. In her sleep she dreams, and she talks her dreams.

At first it irritated him because it kept him up. It irritated him because it was the sound of her stress, too, the images of the restaurant seething up at night like the smoke on her clothes, in fragments and jarring words. It made him conscious of the small room, its dampness, its basement walls.

He would light a cigarette, which he isn't allowed to do, and listen and cough and still she wouldn't wake up. And as he listened he realized that it wasn't just the sound of her stress, it wasn't what he thought at all. Now he listens every night, and thinks, and sleeps when she is at work in the day.

She is telling stories in her sleep. They must be stories she is dreaming, but they don't have the incoherence of dreams. They are real stories, stories he can follow. She narrates them in a voice that wavers, goes up and down, low and monotone and then suddenly squeaking, as if she is doing different characters. Sometimes she shouts or moans. Sometimes the stories have definite endings, and then she starts moving her body around as if looking for something, until she wakes with a jerk. Sometimes they just trail off.

They are strange, though; they have the unpredictability of dreams, and the metamorphoses and the juxtapositions. She has characters who seem to be from medieval fairy tales — the baker, the squire, the princess, the ruffian — and people from her life: Scottie the bartender, Mr Electrician, the Subwayman. There are policemen and office towers, and murders and tea parties and even wars — there is a feud between two groups called the Motmots and the Nipas; Eddie is not sure who or what they are. The princess discusses them in her garden, a garden which is like the real one outside the high window, the garden that belongs to the people upstairs.

It is amazing how they all link up somehow. They are like rock videos with stories.

Eddie imagines how they would be described if they were published. Someone would suggest drugs, of course: a hallucinatory Brothers Grimm for the modern age. Like Tom Wolfe on acid.

He laughs at this one. He thinks about this as he smokes and listens.

In the mornings she is groggy, distant. She makes coffee and reprimands him for smoking, because she can smell it. He asks her if she remembers her dreams, and she laughs and says no, she never can, she has always thought she doesn't dream at all. She thinks it's a hoax, dreaming, that other people just make theirs up. She puts on her waitressing shoes and tells him to go out and do something today, and he tells her he has a meeting with Rick about the recording studio they plan to open, if only they can get the financing. They have met about this before.

When Ellen comes home she is wet; it is raining. Instead of washing it off, the rain has trapped the cigarette smoke to her like adhesive. It is as if the rain itself is liquid smoke. Eddie is not home. She makes herself tea and turns on the television. She doesn't know when she started doing this: she never watched television while she was at university, or even for years afterwards. For years, when she lived with a theatre troupe, and later, when she lived with a composer named Clarence and was taking dance and pottery classes, she did not have a television at all. Eddie brought the television when he moved in with her. And now, she thinks, she doesn't read enough. She always thought that reading would help advance her creative career, when she was thinking all the time about what her career was. She still does, from time to time. Eddie enters, banging things and dropping things, and she says, "You're home early."

"So are you," he says, bending over the big box he has dropped. The cardboard leaves have popped open.

"What is that?"

"Oh, it's a . . ." He stops talking to fumble with the box, take his coat off; he doesn't remember starting sentences sometimes.

"In the box."

"Oh, it's a . . ." The coat hook comes off the coat rack. "*Fucking* thing. I hate this fucking thing so much. I'm going to rip the whole fucking thing from —"

Ellen has walked to the box, opened it; there is some kind of machine inside, an old tape recorder with the two big reels. "What's this?"

"Oh, it's a reel-to-reel Rick had. I'm borrowing it for a while."

"Why?"

"Ah. I'm going to try to . . ." He is trying to plug the dowel back into the hole in the coat rack. "Maybe a little glue would hold it for a while."

She turns back to the television, sits on the sofa.

"*You* know," he says, as if irritated that she is no longer paying attention. "For listening to demos."

"Whose demos?"

"You know. That people send us. You know. For the record label."

"Oh."

"You know. We're really trying to get started on this. It's for real."

"Well that's great. That's good." She thinks about this for a second. He has padded into the kitchenette in his socks. "How will people know, though?"

"Know what?"

"Well, to send you demos. How will they know you're a recording company?"

Eddie pauses, and she knows the pause is a tense one. "Listen," he says finally. "I know it's very easy to make fun when someone is just starting out. And that's all this is. It's a start. But I'm pretty serious about it."

"I'm sorry." She stands, walks over to him. "I am. I know you are."

"And so is Rick."

"I know he is. I'm sorry." She puts her hands on his shoulders. She does feel guilty.

"You have to start somewhere, you know."

She hugs him and he stiffens. "Listen, I'm very proud of you, starting this. It's very brave. I couldn't —"

"We're putting the word out, you know? Word will spread around that we're listening to stuff, and then the stuff will start coming in."

"That's terrific."

She makes tea and they both sit in front of the TV, but she is sad as she steps over the box again, the dusty tape recorder which is obviously old. It belongs in someone's rec room. Now they are a home recording studio. Good for Eddie. At least he is more innocent than she is.

He is yawning unstoppably. "Haven't been getting enough sleep," he says.

"I know," she says. "I don't know what's wrong with you. I wish you would go to see Mister Koo. He gave me some stuff for my ankle that —"

But Eddie has already lumbered to the bed for a nap. He puts the tape recorder on the bedside table, and Ellen doesn't say anything, even though it covers the whole top and is probably going to fall off, and even if it doesn't she knows it is going to just sit there forever.

She goes to sleep easily that night, even though he wakes her a couple of times, clicking and fussing with his new machine.

The demo tapes are piling up on the desk by the phone, a desk they were supposed to share but which has become Eddie's desk. Ellen isn't sure where the tapes are coming from, or where he quickly files them away to, and she is not keen on the tiny apartment becoming more filled with junk, but she is pleased that he is doing something and says nothing about it. He doesn't seem to want to talk about it, either; he won't say if any of the tapes are any good. She takes this as a good sign too, because he has talked too much about all his other projects since the band dissolved, and they have never come to anything.

He is still not sleeping at night, and takes long naps in the day, sometimes even in the mornings. He has bought a second-hand typewriter and is sometimes typing on it when she comes home from work, but he always rips the paper out and stuffs it in a file and won't show her what he's doing. Sometimes he types at night, when she is sleeping. She has learned to find the clacking of the keys soothing; it leads her like the rhythmic sound of train wheels into her dreamless sleep where the restaurant doesn't bother her.

One day she finds him reading a magazine called *Writers' Market*.

"I don't know," he says. "Just curious."

"Are you writing stories?"

"Sort of," he says. "Yeah."

"Eddie," she says, sitting beside him. "You know, I thought you were. And I don't know why you're so shy about it. I think that's wonderful. I really do. You never told me you had any interest in writing." Something about this discovery makes her want to cry.

Eddie is unusually unwilling to discuss his new project. This surprises her, but she has known many creative people and knows that it is sometimes this way, that you can't discuss something creative while you are working on it, and so she leaves it alone. Still, it is unlike Eddie. It is all so unlike Eddie. Maybe this is why he is so shy about it: he is embarrassed to be unlike himself.

In the next weeks she tries to be as supportive as she can about it. She buys him literary quarterlies and typing paper. He enjoys this attention, and he reads the magazines closely. It's the first time she's seen him read anything for longer than ten minutes. He seems genuinely interested. Still, he can't type when she's around. He seems to have lost interest in the record label, which is fine with her. She thinks this is more realistic. It makes her excited and fragile at the same time; she's not sure why.

One day she comes home early and Eddie is not there. Perhaps he is out with Rick. She takes off her coat as slowly as she can, forces herself to put on the kettle before she goes to his desk. A page is in the typewriter; more are scattered around. It is a story, a sort of fantastic one. It is hard to read because Eddie's typing is so bad; half of each page is misspelled and crossed out. It is mostly description, of a city of sparkling towers, and a little girl who sells herbal tea in a sort of market. Perhaps it is science fiction. She is getting interested in this little girl, who seems familiar to her, as if Eddie has based her on a character she has already read, and half aware of a stomachache she is getting, a thickening in her neck like nausea, when Eddie crashes in, dropping things and banging things, and before she has moved fully away from the desk he says, "*Hey.*" He strides to the desk and rips the sheet out of the typewriter.

"I couldn't help it," she says. "It was just sitting there. You shouldn't leave it out if —"

"You're home early." He is gathering up papers, straightening them in a folder. He hasn't taken his coat off.

"Sorry. I didn't read much. What I did read I thought was marvellous. It's wonderful. You should send them out." She sits on the sofa because she is still reeling from a sick feeling, as if her insides were hollowing out and going cold. Her head begins to pound.

"You think."

"I don't know why you're so hostile about it. We all have . . ." She closes her eyes against her headache. "I wish more people would realize that they have stories to tell. I think we all . . ." She can't go on because her throat is lumpy, as if she is going to cry. She gets up. She doesn't know why she is feeling so crazy these days. Maybe it's because she doesn't believe what she's telling Eddie; she doesn't believe it herself.

"I was going to go out and get us falafel for dinner." She has to get out and cry in the street so he won't see her. If she cries for no reason like this he gets upset.

After dinner they watch TV and she is calmer, although she is thinking about his story. Her desire to read more about the little girl in the marketplace is physical; she can't keep still. She hasn't brought it up because she knows he won't let her.

She is still thinking about it when they go to bed. She thinks that if she can stay awake until he falls asleep then she can creep to the desk and read the rest without waking him. So they both lie awake. She tries talking. "Is it a novel or short stories?" she says. "You can at least tell me that."

"Sort of short stories," he says. "Aren't you sleepy?"

"No. Are you?"

"Yes. Very."

"Sorry. I'll shut up then. Goodnight."

A minute later she says, "What do you mean, sort of?"

"What?"

"Sort of short stories. What does that mean?"

He sighs dramatically. "They're kind of related."

"They're linked."

"Yes."

"Oh. Cool. That's interesting. It's a good gimmick. Are you thinking about who you're going to send them to?"

He pauses a long time before answering quietly, "Yes."

"Good," she says, equally quietly. "Then let's do it. I'll help you. I'll send out the letters, do the typing, whatever. I'm good at that. I did a lot of temping."

He thinks about this in silence and then says, "Don't you have to be up early?"

She says, "Yeah. Sorry. Goodnight."

"Goodnight."

She listens to him breathing and shifting around. Her thoughts are coming more confusedly now. She has pictures of a city with glittering towers, and then suddenly feels nausea. She wants to sleep. She knows she has to stay awake, outlast him. Now he is fidgeting with his tape recorder again, clicking buttons. "Put that thing away," she murmurs. "You're not going to do any work with it now."

"No," he whispers. "I didn't mean to keep you up. Go to sleep."

"You go to sleep."

"Shh." He puts the machine back on the bedside table and is quiet.

Ellen waits, struggling against the images that move. When she feels herself sinking, she moves her body.

Finally she hears his breathing slow and thicken. His body has gone slack. She touches the back of his neck and he does not move. Carefully, she slips out of the bed. She shakes off sleep. She puts on her housecoat and steps into the living room in the darkness, her hands stretched out in front of her like radar. She trips on magazines and still he does not wake.

She stands at his desk and switches on the tin lamp. She opens drawers until she finds the folder. She opens it to the description of the city, the little girl.

Ellen squints against the appalling typing. She is not surprised at this. Nor is she surprised by the style, which is colloquial; it is as if Eddie is telling the story to someone in a bar. She is pleased by this: at least he is not trying anything too literary. And she is impressed by how natural it sounds. (It was Clarence who told her about colloquial speech, and that it was not easy to make things sound colloquial.) It is perhaps not terribly original. She can't shake the feeling of cliché, as if she has read similar stories. Although she knows she hasn't.

She is hardly aware that her stomachache has returned. She notices it as she reads about a princess, high in an office tower, who is looking out over the city. The princess's name is Eloise. As she reads this name, the nausea tugs at her so suddenly she has to sit down. Eloise sounds irritatingly derivative to her; she has read it in another story somewhere.

This upsets her so much she feels weepy again, and then crazy and stupid again. She checked her pills early in the day and found she was almost at the end of her cycle, which would explain it. She is craving a cigarette, which is particularly strange since she quit three years ago, and it rarely takes her like this any more. Perhaps she is just envious of Eddie, his writing.

She tried writing, in university, in a creative writing class, but she found the mutual criticism sessions stressful; no one encouraged her to continue.

She can't read any more, and moves to the sofa where she curls into a ball and lets herself cry a little. She feels better after this, and sleepy. She can't move.

Eddie wakes up. He has been dreaming of bands, loud rehearsals with amps that keep cutting out. He wakes with a jerk and says, "Shit," out loud, because he remembers that he was trying to stay awake, that he never set up the reel-to-reel, and then he realizes that Ellen is not in bed. He sits up and he hears her talking from the living room.

He stands and walks into the living room the same way she did, with his hands as paths through the darkness. He finds her asleep on the couch and talking. She is moving as she talks, arching her back and kicking her bare feet. Her fists are clenched. Her nightdress has risen around her waist; her pubic hair looks stark and ugly. He does not touch her. He sits and listens.

It is violent, this story. There is rain and sleet, and Princess Eloise has turned mean; she is shouting at someone in a caustic and condescending way, a servant or maid. Eddie leans close to listen for the maid's name; it keeps getting slurred.

Eddie goes to his desk, where the lamp is still on. His blotchy pages are scattered all over. Some are thrown on the floor.

He sorts them, puts them back in the file. He goes to Ellen and picks her up. He carries her back to bed. She does not wake. He does not tape her tonight.

They say nothing at breakfast. Ellen looks grey; her face sags. Eddie is thinking that she should wash her hair more often and she says, "Eddie, I'm sorry I read your story." She is speaking with effort, as if she is still tired. "But I'm not sorry. I've been thinking about it all the time. And I think it's good. I think it's *really* good."

Eddie says nothing.

"And I want to help you. I'm going to get you published."

Eddie is chewing on the inside of his cheek and frowning. "I don't know —"

"Why don't you want me to help you?"

Eddie says slowly, "I don't know if you want to help me publish these stories."

"Why not? Because you think I'm jealous?"

"No." He shakes his head firmly. "No."

"Then why?"

He takes a long time before replying, "I don't know."

"Well that's not good enough." She stands and collects their cups decisively.

Over the next weeks she reads all his stories in the evenings, despite the sick feeling she has, the flu or whatever it is she has picked up. Eddie watches TV, frowning. She retypes them all and corrects the spelling. She also suggests titles, as Eddie says he is no good at titles. She smiles at this, because she finds it very easy to choose a title for each story. The title just comes to her.

Sometimes she fixes the grammar, but she does not change the style, rarely dares change a word unless it is incorrectly spelled. She is very respectful of artists. She types the cover letters and chooses the magazines and sends them out.

Four weeks later, a small quarterly called *Coelacanth Apartments* sends him an eager letter. Ellen has researched this journal carefully: it is run by students at the left-wing university in the suburbs, and it has a reputation for violent sex stories. They would like to publish Eddie's story "The Metal Snake," and they will pay him one hundred dollars for it. The magazine will appear in three months. "The Metal Snake" was the very first story she sent out.

Eddie is less excited about this than he should be, Ellen thinks. They go out for Thai food and he seems distracted and worried and not overjoyed as she would be. Perhaps he finds the possibility of rejection stressful; she knows she would. She can't eat much because of her stomach problem. Perhaps she is stressed, too.

So she soothes him and sends out more stories.

Three more are quickly accepted, one by a conservative international quarterly called *Quod Libet*. Ellen has to explain to him how significant this is. They agonize together over the wording of the "bio note" which will appear at the back of the journal. Eddie is insistent that the name of his first band, the Shards, be mentioned, as well as the fact that their video once appeared on MTV. He is starting to be impressed by himself.

Random, the art magazine, picks up one, and *Haze* picks up another. These are good because they are both monthlies, and they pay much more than the quarterlies. Eddie buys himself a second-hand computer and a printer with the first cheque; a navy cashmere sports jacket with the second. Ellen loves the jacket; she almost cries just touching it.

By the time they appear in print, Eddie has a new stack of stories to retype. Ellen is tired, spending all her time at the restaurant or at home in front of the computer. A literary agent who read the story in *Coelacanth* calls, asking for Eddie. She wants to know if he has enough stories for a book, as she's on her way to a publishing trade fair in Berlin. Eddie hands the phone to Ellen, who takes down the address.

She has taken up smoking. She doesn't know why, or even when exactly it started again. She is proud of Eddie, she knows she is; still his success is somehow stressful. Perhaps it is the hours she is working. She has trouble rising from the blackness in the mornings, and when she does she still feels tired. She has been drinking Mister Koo's bitter tea for her stomach problem, but she has decided to see a Western doctor as well; she won't admit this to her friend Julie, who put her on to Mister Koo. She is eating less and losing weight.

Eddie's agent Vanna is doing more of her work for her. Vanna sells a book of his stories to Gloosecap House, a good publisher, not too commercial but not too small, a serious one. Eddie wants to call the collection *Dreams*, but Vanna thinks this is a little fey and obvious; she suggests *The Crystal Age*, after one of the stories called "The Crystal Garden." Ellen thinks that *Dreams* is a perfect title, and if anything *The Crystal Age* is more fey, but she can't explain this clearly enough to Vanna.

Vanna is good: she makes sure everybody hears about the deal, and it is reported on before the book is even out, in *Reams and Reams*, the publishing industry magazine.

It is only when the monthly city magazine, *Edge*, hears about this book that Eddie becomes actually famous. A young editor at *Edge* named Julian read "The Crystal Garden" in *Quod Libet* and loved it. When he reads that Eddie has a book deal, he knows that he must make it clear that he was on to this guy before everyone else was. The editor bets a lot on Eddie, in a kind of pre-emptive strike: he convinces the editor-in-chief of Eddie's imminent celebrity, of Eddie's appeal to their young urban readers, which there are never enough of; he speaks of gritty fantasy and magic realism for North America, of street-level literature and folklore in a technological age. Nobody is doing serialized fiction any more; why not? It gets readers hooked and encourages subscriptions. The young editor tells the story of the crowds lining the docks in nineteenth-century America, waiting for the arrival of the ships bearing Dickens's next chapter. Why not?

The editor-in-chief is intimidated by any talk of cybervision and young people, and gives his assent. The young editor calls Vanna and offers Eddie a serial. A story every month, with recurring characters in each, like a kind of soap opera.

Eddie is finally excited; he speaks with more confidence about his writing. He accepts the offer with the ease of a craftsman who expects business; in his dealings with *Edge* he is majestically cool. Ellen is less excited: it just means more typing for her. Still, the money is good. The thought occurs to her that eventually this hobby of Eddie's may permit her to leave the restaurant.

She is feeling so sick these days that she sometimes asks Julie to take a shift or two for her. She has had blood tests and ultrasounds and barium swallows that all returned normal. She is sitting at home one day in her housecoat, smoking, and she turns on the TV because she knows Eddie is being interviewed that afternoon on a daytime talk show.

Eddie is slouched in his chair, wearing his navy cashmere jacket. He has cut his hair short, at her insistence, and he looks handsome. The host of the show is a woman in her forties; she is bubbling all over him. He is having a hard time answering her questions: he pauses for long seconds before answering, and then comes out with some wisecrack about how he doesn't know anything, he doesn't even know why he is there. He is grinning, so it is obviously a joke; the host finds it charming. She keeps coming back to the idea of "working-class imagination," as that is the role Eddie has been happy with in his previous interviews.

He is not really of working-class origin, Ellen knows, but he has never been very good with language, and it works out to the same thing. It is an easy way of explaining it. She has stopped wondering about where Eddie comes up with his fantastic ideas; Eddie doesn't seem to know, and she knows it often works that way. The ideas just come to you; that is Eddie's gift.

The host is asking him about Princess Eloise — she just loves this character. Every time Ellen hears the name Eloise, she feels another wriggle of nausea. She lights another cigarette.

"The princess," Eddie is saying with much concentration, "is in charge of her own destiny."

Ellen stands up, stumbling forward, and runs to the bathroom. She falls to her knees and vomits into the toilet repeatedly. Then she sits on the floor, hugging her knees and shivering.

Eddie comes home to find her in bed, pale. She tells him she was sick. He makes her eat some soup. She falls asleep early.

Soon she is dreaming and talking. He sits beside her on the bed and listens but does not tape her because the narrative is too violent and incoherent; there is sex and swearing. Ellen sweats and writhes. The princess is being shrewish again. Now she is ugly, too: she has cut all her hair off. She is mocking someone again, swearing and threatening. This time Eddie can hear the name clearly. It is the name of a new character in the stories. The princess is shouting at someone called Ellen.

Eddie stands up and lights himself a cigarette. He sits on the sofa in darkness. He knows he has to think hard about this. He has been putting it off but he knows he has to do it. He meant to tell Ellen at the beginning but then it got out of hand. It would be hard to explain now. But he can't stand to see her sick. It is spooking him, he thinks, *I am spooked.* He thinks that when he first started this he wanted Ellen to be the star. But he knew — he had a hunch — that she wouldn't be able to do it if she knew what she was doing. You can't dream consciously, he knows that. What was he supposed to do, say okay, now dream, *go?* He knows that wouldn't have worked. Ellen isn't good at pressure.

He was going to tell her once it got going, show her how much talent she had locked up inside her. He doesn't know how it got so out of hand. It was never meant to make her sick. It was never meant to ruin her life. He wants everything to go back to how it was before, before he had to do all these interviews. The interviews are freaking him out, too. He doesn't know what to say, and they seem to love it. It freaks him out that Ellen is watching him at home; he knows it bothers her and she doesn't know why.

Ellen's voice is humming in the background. Now she is imitating a police siren. Eddie grits his teeth. He decides he needs some time to think about this, some time alone. He decides to take the next day off; he won't transcribe tapes, even though Ellen will be out of the apartment. He needs to get back to the way things were. He'll go find Rick tomorrow, maybe spend some time with him at Helium the way he used to. He needs to think this out.

Ellen utters a little shriek, and he jumps. *Boy*, he thinks. *I am spooked.*

In the morning Ellen is still feeling sick. She calls Julie and convinces her to take her shift. She is so filled with love and gratitude to Julie for taking her shift that she almost cries. Julie is always like this. Ellen wishes she were more like Julie.

Eddie seems sad, too. He announces he needs a break, says he's not going to work today. He says he's going to go find Rick, talk about some new demo tapes he has. Ellen doesn't question this. She's too tired to wonder about it. She thinks Eddie probably just doesn't want to spend the day cooped up with her in the apartment, and she doesn't blame him. She knows she is being a drag these days.

She watches TV for most of the morning and smokes uncontrollably, although she knows it makes her sicker. She realizes she is in a rut, something bad is happening to her. She should get help, snap out of it.

She sits up and stubs out her cigarette and says, "Snap out of it."

She looks around the apartment and realizes it is filthy. It is covered with papers and magazines. She has not noticed this for weeks.

She switches off the TV and stands. If she gets dressed and cleans up, it will be a start. She dresses painfully; the nausea has turned into something like cramps.

She begins stacking papers and folding clothes. It makes her feel a little better. She hauls out the vacuum cleaner and sucks up runways of dust. She is imposing order, she thinks.

She comes to Eddie's desk and hesitates. It is a disaster, as usual; it's just a big recycling bin. She can't touch it, of course; she knows this. But she knows that he won't notice if she moves the old Coke can and the dirty cereal bowl and the rag that could be a sock. She can't help it. The more she moves, the more junk she finds — old Lego pieces, things that he couldn't possibly need — and the more she wants to clean.

She stacks papers into files. There is no room on the desk for them, so she opens a drawer. It is full of paper. She opens another drawer and finds the old reel-to-reel tape recorder in it. She had thought this was in the garage. She didn't know he still used it. In another drawer are the stacks of tapes.

She knows that this is dangerous.

She pulls out the tape recorder and one of the tapes, at random. The tapes all have labels on them now: dates. Some of the dates are quite recent.

It takes her a few minutes to figure out how to thread the tape, partly because it is complicated and partly because her fingers shake from all the cigarettes.

She clicks the rotary dial to Play and she hears hiss and banging, then a soft voice. As soon as she hears the voice she knows the story it is telling. It is not a story she has typed yet, but she knows it, she can tell the rest of it.

She stops the machine after two minutes.

She knows her own voice.

She sits in silence for a long time. Her stomach is calm. Her eyes are wide open. She stares at the wall. She realizes now that she has, in fact, understood all along.

She thinks of all the stories she has typed, tries to remember them in order. She thinks of all of Eddie's incoherent explanations. How she has always known what was going to happen next. She has always known.

She sits for most of the afternoon, almost without blinking. Eddie's stories are hers. She does not even smoke.

She doesn't know what to do about it. The thought of confronting Eddie exhausts her. She doesn't know what good it would do. For a while she considers pretending she has not understood, going on as before. Eddie is better at interviews than she would be, anyway.

When she is hungry she gets up and calls Julie at work. She is not crying; she is very calm and clear. Julie says she's off in an hour and will call her back.

This doesn't help. Ellen knows what Julie will advise: to confront him, sue the bastard, take your stories back. But Ellen is not good at fights. She has to think about it for a while. It always takes her a while to muster anger when she has been hurt. It is a different phase. She has to hide first.

She feels tired and lies down but can't sleep. After an hour she begins to feel it, the anger: it is like a prickling in her limbs. She can't lie still.

She gets up and calls a locksmith. She is going to change the locks before Eddie comes home. At least she can think about it alone.

The lawyer tells her it's a difficult case. Eddie did in fact type the stories out; Ellen had never made an effort to do so. And she can't prove that her voice on the tapes is not just her reading out Eddie's stories, should Eddie choose to deny everything. The lawyer says he will take her case, but she should be aware that she has a fight on her hands.

"Tell me about it," says Ellen. "I'm having a fight on my hands just getting legal aid. There's a waiting list, did you know? It was a fight just to get the forms."

"Ah," says the lawyer. He sits back and looks out the window. "Yes, I know."

Ellen sits with a pen and a pad of paper. Eddie took the computer when he moved his stuff out. She could never write at a computer anyway. She writes down the names of the characters she remembers. She stares up to the little window above the fridge, the only one in this end of the apartment. It is level with the ground, the asphalt of the driveway that runs down the side of the house. She sees snowboots passing. She tries to concentrate. She has a few pictures in her head, but she doesn't know if they are from reading Eddie's stories or if they are memories of dreams. She still thinks of them as Eddie's stories.

Julie has relented on the lawsuit, allowed her to give up. Ellen was never very big on revenge. Julie counselled her to keep a pad of paper and a pen by her bed, to write down her dreams the moment she wakes; it is a well-known method.

Ellen wakes from the blackness and remembers nothing. She picks up the pad and doodles.

She calls Eddie at Rick's, where he is staying, and asks for the reel-to-reel. He does not argue or ask why she needs it. Eddie has been very quiet since he stopped publishing. He leaves the tape recorder and some blank tape in between her front doors; he does not ring the bell.

She is nervous the first night she tries it. She wears a flannel nightdress, drinks chamomile tea before bed. She props the microphone on a book, on Eddie's empty pillow. She wonders how he used to do it. She threads a tape that should last three hours, sets it to record, closes her eyes.

The tape machine hisses. Something grinds as the wheels turn. She opens her eyes and looks at the square of artificial light in the window up by the ceiling. She knows she will not sleep for hours, and so she turns the machine off.

She does not sleep for hours. She tries not to move, as if lying in wait for the images. She dozes off from time to time, and when she wakes with a start she reaches over and switches the machine on again. Then she can hear it listening to her.

She wakes in the morning in silence. The machine is off. She remembers fragments of dreams, being late and lost in the labyrinthine and crowded passages of an ocean liner which is bound for the wrong destination. This agitates her, as she never remembers her dreams. She gets up, makes coffee, trying to calm herself before listening to the tape.

When she finally sits and rewinds it, her heart is pounding. She listens to the whole thing: it is mostly silent, except for a few moments of speech which makes no sense. It is gibberish, random phrases, just like everyone else's sleep-talking. She listens to the very end but hears nothing coherent.

She tells herself she shouldn't be upset. Once she gets into the routine of it she will relax enough to dream properly. She does some yoga to calm down. She cries anyway.

Two weeks pass and she has given up on the tape. She works as many shifts as she can without collapsing, and spends the rest of the time in the apartment. She can't sleep. She knows she is sleeping a little every night, but it is not restful sleep. She can't dream. The tape has recorded nothing. She has had so little sleep that she can't concentrate. She is watching TV and smoking too much. Julie has told her frankly she is worried about her. Ellen has stopped answering the phone because she is sick of Julie's efforts to get her to go out, to the Y or to the Gelateria, to go rollerblading with her. Ellen can only see all this as idiotic. She is crying too much to go out anyway.

She has tried putting on the Wavescape CD Julie lent her, and extra-relaxing tea from Mister Koo and hot milk before bed, even though she normally avoids dairy. She wishes she liked alcohol, so she could drink herself into a stupor every night. She has tried buying a bottle of whisky but she could only drink two small glasses before feeling sick. And that night was particularly bad; she didn't even doze.

She feels she has tried everything. She has considered calling Eddie and asking him to come back.

She does not need to consider this for long, because he comes back uninvited. He just knocks at the door one afternoon. He must have been asking Julie about her, because he knows that she would normally be at work at this time. She lets him in, in silence; she wants to explain to him that she is too tired to express surprise, but she doesn't even do that.

He tries to hug her and she lets him. She feels sad to smell his cologne; it is fairly recent, this cologne thing, and besides, she bought it for him. He wears a soft leather coat and dark wool trousers, leather boots that look Italian. He's carrying a laptop computer in a leather case. She says, "You look great."

"So do you."

"No, I don't."

"Can I sit down?"

She shrugs, and they both sit down.

"You look tired," he says softly. He is leaning forward and looking at her with big earnest eyes. "Are you okay?"

"Thank you for asking," she says, with sudden tears in her eyes. She doesn't know whether to scream at him or curl up in his lap.

"How is it going?" he says. "Are you — are you doing your own —"

"No. I can't sleep."

"Oh." There is a silence. "I'm sorry."

She laughs a little.

"I'm sorry for everything. I mean it."

"Thank you. It doesn't matter."

"Ellen, you look terrible. Is there anything I can —"

"So what are you up to?" She lights a cigarette.

He opens his hands, palms upwards, raises his eyebrows, as if to say where do I start? Indeed, there is too much for him to describe. He is turning down all the requests for new stories, but he has stayed in publishing; he has found that the business agrees with him. He first got involved with the student magazine, *Coelacanth*, as a business manager. Now he is overseeing their on-line magazine, and others have approached him to do the same. He is hoping to launch an on-line magazine of his own, more like a sort of shopping catalogue. He has found you can make money at it, that he is good at it. He spreads his hands along the back of the sofa as he speaks, opening his arms wide as if to welcome the world to his breast.

Ellen is glad, honestly glad for him. She says, "That's great. That's *terrific*. It's so much better for you than . . ."

"Yeah. I guess."

She is silent for a second. "Do you miss it at all? Being a . . ."

"A writer?" He smiles.

"Yes."

He shrugs. "Yes. Of course I do. I was famous. It was fun. I miss it."

She nods. Her eyes close. "Eddie. I'm so tired."

He moves closer to her, puts his arm around her. "I know. I know you are. I want to help."

She sighs. "Thanks."

"Ellen. Please. Let me. Let me help you. You need sleep."

"I know I need sleep."

"Come here." He pulls her to him and she does not resist. His shoulder is soft and leather-smelling. He strokes her hair. "Come on. Let me put you to bed."

She does not resist as he leads her to the bed, lifts her arms above her head to pull off her sweatshirt. He undresses her gently. She is suddenly sleepy. He hands her her flannel nightdress.

She climbs into bed and pulls the duvet up to her chin and whimpers, "Eddie, this is weird. It's the middle of the afternoon."

He sits on the edge of the bed and says, "Shhh. You need sleep."

"I can't. I can't sleep."

"I'll help you." He is unzipping the case around his laptop computer.

"What are you doing?" Her eyes are closing. The bed is warm. The duvet is heavy on her.

"Shhh."

She hears the beep and whirring as the computer powers up. Eddie's hand is stroking her hair and she feels sleepier than she has all week. She hears the clack of keys. "What are you doing?"

"I'm going to do some typing. You go to sleep."

"No." The room is moving around her. She sees pictures of the ocean liner, the glittering city, Princess Eloise. Princess Eloise's face is wounded, or in shock. "No," she says.

"It's okay." His voice is distant.

Ellen may have replied to this, but she doesn't know. She doesn't know if she is talking or not.

"It's okay," comes the voice, over the clicking keys. The keys are the sound of rain or travel. They are all she can hear. She can see the clicks and hear them. They are black and velvet. They are all around her, enveloping her like water, and she is sinking beneath it.

Acknowledgements

"Young Men" was first published in *Toronto Life*. Part of "Party Going" first appeared in *Vice Versa* and was published in full in the *New Quarterly*. "Home" was first published in *Flare*. "Chez Giovanni" was first published in the *Malahat Review*. "Dreams" is forthcoming in the *Antigonish Review*.

Many thanks to the above journals. This book was written with financial assistance from the Toronto Arts Council, to whom I am grateful. Thanks also to the staff of the Bar Italia, Katherine Bruce for help with "Chez Giovanni," my editors Maya Mavjee and Martha Kanya-Forstner for their insightful analyses, Anne McDermid and Bethany Gibson, and Ceri Marsh for everything else.

About the Author

Russell Smith is a well-known journalist and novelist. His 1994 bestseller, *How Insensitive*, was shortlisted for the Governor General's Award, the Chapters/Books in Canada First Novel Award, and Ontario's Trillium Book Award. His second novel, *Noise*, published in 1998, received widespread attention and critical acclaim. An accomplished journalist, Smith's articles have been published in the *Globe and Mail*, *Toronto Life*, *Flare*, *Details*, and *Travel and Leisure*. His story "Party Going," won the 1997 National Magazine Award for fiction. Smith currently writes a weekly column on men and fashion for the *Globe and Mail*. He lives in Toronto.